Boats and

CW00736173

Dune House Cozy Mystery Series

Cindy Bell

ISBN-13: 978-1501050190

ISBN-10: 1501050192

More Cozy Mysteries by Cindy Bell

Dune House Cozy Mystery Series

Seaside Secrets

Boats and Bad Guys

Heavenly Highland Inn Cozy Mystery Series

Murdering the Roses

Dead in the Daisies

Killing the Carnations

Drowning the Daffodils

Suffocating the Sunflowers

Table of Contents

Chapter One

The high-pitched sound of the drill was enough to send a flock of seagulls gathered on the sand, straight up into the sky above the ocean. The sound was coming from deep within Dune House, a majestic home that was one of the oldest buildings in the small seaside town of Garber. Inside the gabled roof and the floor-to-ceiling windows, Suzie Allen was watching with a studious expression as her best friend, Mary, continued to drill holes into the front wall. They were in the main sitting area just inside the front door of the home Suzie had inherited. Together the two friends were renovating the neglected home so it could once again be used as a bed and breakfast. Suzie tilted her head to one side, and then to the other. After leaving her long time career as an investigative journalist she became an interior decorator. This made her very critical of every choice she made.

1

During the renovations of the house, Suzie preferred to supervise, as opposed to undertake, certain aspects of the renovation. Mary had a little more experience using power tools, as she often had to do her own home improvements on her old house while her husband had neglected their family. The neglect had finally come to a head which resulted in her being recently divorced. Suzie on the other hand, had never had a taste for marriage, and had pursued a career in investigative journalism while Mary raised her children. Though the two women had taken very different paths in life, they had never lost their affection for each other, nor had either failed to support the other. Now, in their fifties they had the opportunity to both work and live together. It was a bit of an adjustment to be under the same roof, but neither woman would have it any other way.

"Are you sure that's the right spot for the painting?" Suzie asked with uncertainty while Mary focused intently on the job at hand. Suzie's original intention after inheriting the old home was to update it, decorate it, and sell it for a nice profit. But once she had become familiar with it, and its place in the town's history, she changed her plans. She decided to open it as a B & B, and along with Mary, run it as a business they could enjoy and share well into their old age. It was in an ideal location positioned right beside the sea on slightly higher ground than the rest of the town which it overlooked. Suzie's late Uncle Harry and Aunt Beverly used to run it as a B & B, but when Aunt Beverly died Uncle Harry closed it to the public and became a recluse.

"If I put any more holes in this wall it's going to look like swiss cheese!" Mary announced with exasperation as she turned off the drill.

"Hmm," Suzie nodded and laughed softly. "I think you're right. I don't know, something about it just isn't working for me," she said with a deep sigh. "This is the first room that our guests will experience and I want everything to be just perfect."

"Well, what do you think it is?" Mary asked as she carefully climbed down from the ladder. "You're the one with an eye for details."

Suzie took a few steps back and stared up at the large, empty wall. It did have a few extra holes poked in it, but the large painting she was hoping to hang there would cover all of those. The painting that was on the floor leaning against the wall was a panoramic view of a seascape. It was beautiful, and the colors mingled well with the muted tones of blue and green that were scattered throughout the room in the carpeting, the paint on the walls, and the furniture.

"It just leaves me feeling unsettled, as if it doesn't belong," Suzie admitted and shook her head.

"I think it's fine," Mary shrugged and put down the drill on a folding table set up beside the ladder. "But I know it will drive you nuts if we hang it. So, why don't we just focus on something else right now?" she suggested. "Sometimes if you stare at something for too long it stumps you."

4

"That's true," Suzie smiled warmly at her friend, who knew her very well. "What would I do without you, Mary?" she asked.

"Well," Mary scrunched up her nose and pulled the hair band out of her silver streaked auburn hair letting it fall against her shoulders and back as she looked up at Suzie. "You'd have a lot less holes, that's for sure."

"Funny gal you are," Suzie winked at her. "I do need to pick up a few things from town. Shall we take a break and see what's going on with the locals?"

"Sure, just give me a minute to get cleaned up," Mary said as she brushed some dust from her shirt.

"Take your time, I need to do something about this hair," Suzie said with a huff and ran her fingers through her brassy blonde hair. She wasn't used to living by the sea, and neither was her hair. The short no fuss no muss cut that had worked in the city, wasn't working so well in her new environment. She paused in the doorway of her room. A shiver ran up along her spine as all of a sudden she felt a sense of being watched. This place did that to her. It seemed as if the walls held many secrets about the past guests that had stayed there. She would often find it hard to believe that the house had been standing for so long. She closed her eyes briefly and dismissed the notion of someone watching her before stepping into the bathroom. She straightened her hair, which she dyed to give her a more youthful and up-to-date look. Then she applied a small amount of mascara to the lashes that framed her bright blue eyes.

Suzie stared in the mirror for a long moment. She was not one to lose confidence with age, she was of the belief that women only grew more beautiful in different ways as they progressed through life. She only wished that she could convince Mary of the same. The divorce had dealt her friend a very hard blow, and Suzie was determined to help her confidence blossom once more. With her own children grown and in college, Mary was no longer a mother on call every hour of the day, and she was no longer a wife. Although both Suzie and Mary saw moving to Garber as a fresh start, Mary still felt a bit lost. However, having the B & B to work on seemed to be helping.

Suzie added some simple gold earrings to her ensemble of straight-legged jeans and a button-down, sleeveless, white blouse. She was enjoying the fact that she didn't have to make an effort to get a tan anymore as she was always on the beach.

Suzie met up with Mary in the hall to find her donning a very large, bright purple, wide-brimmed sunhat.

"What in the world is that monstrosity?" Suzie asked as she looked at the hat.

"Well, I want to protect my skin from drying out which sun protection cream doesn't do very well," Mary replied with a slight shrug. "I've heard there is a much higher risk of getting sun damage to your skin when you live near the ocean."

"I've heard there's a much lower risk of romance when potential dates only see a hat," Suzie replied and bent the brim of the hat upward so that Mary's face was out of the shadows. "There that's better," Suzie sighed with relief. "Can't hide that beautiful smile."

Mary smiled in response to Suzie's comment, but she shook her head firmly. "I'm not looking for any dates, Suzie. I need a little more time alone I think."

"Don't you think being alone for most of your marriage is enough time?" Suzie pressed as tenderly as she could. She was always blunt with Mary, and Mary seemed to love her for it, but she knew that this was a very sensitive situation.

"You're right," Mary said quietly as her smile faded. "Perhaps I've just become accustomed to being alone. There's something beautiful about solitude, you know."

"You see beauty, I see an empty chair," Suzie

explained as she looped her arm through Mary's and they walked towards the door of Dune House. "Sometimes I think it will always be empty."

"It could be worse," Mary pointed out with a light wink. "Trust me."

"Well, no matter how our lives have changed, and our paths have veered off in unexpected directions, the important thing to me is that it led us to be here together, which is the best 'happily ever after' I could ever think of," Suzie said as she closed the door behind them.

"Aw Suz, you always say the sweetest things," Mary giggled and batted her eyes at Suzie. "Are you sure you don't want to marry me?"

"Well, we are already living together," Suzie mused and as they got into the car they both dissolved into giggles. That was one of the things Suzie loved most about being around Mary, no matter what they were doing, they could always find the humor in it.

Mary fiddled with the radio as Suzie drove

along the winding road that led into the town square. It had its tourist traps, but was mostly filled with quaint individually owned shops. The town of Garber's simple beauty and relaxed lifestyle was a very well kept secret.

"I think we should have a nice open house party for the locals when we're done fixing Dune House up," Mary suggested with a smile. "What do you think?"

"What do I always think, Mary?" Suzie asked as she turned onto the main street that headed through the center of town.

"I don't know, what?" Mary asked hesitantly.

"That you're brilliant," Suzie grinned at her and Mary laughed.

"Well, at least someone thinks so," she replied with a smile.

When they reached town Suzie noticed that the main street was dotted with white tents. People were walking along the sidewalks, stopping in the tents and then moving along.

"Looks like they're having some kind of fair," Mary said as she looked out the window.

"Sure does," Suzie replied and narrowed her eyes as she peered into one of the tents. "Oh, I think we're in luck, Mary! Let's pull in here," she pointed to the parking lot beside the library that was being used as the main parking area for the fair.

"Why, what did you spot?" Mary asked with excitement.

"It's an art fair," Suzie declared as they left the car behind and headed for the white tents. "Maybe we'll find a better picture for the front room."

Mary groaned teasingly. "A better picture? Why does that make me think I'm going to be drilling more holes?"

"Shh," Suzie waved her hand and pretended not to hear her friend's concern. She locked the car and they began walking towards the tents. Suzie smiled at a few people, but the locals were still getting used to her. They offered polite smiles in return, but hurried along. Suzie had found most of the people in the town to be friendly enough, especially since her cousin, Jason, was a police officer, but they didn't exactly open up to outsiders. She was okay with that, as she rather preferred her privacy.

The tents along the street were filled with all kinds of interesting items, vendors had their tables set up to display their wares. There were many things to see, from handcrafted jewelry, to shell art made from finds on the local beach, to art created by someone's cat.

"Would you look at this?" Mary giggled as she pointed to a large painting covered in cat paw prints. "How's that for the front room?" she suggested with mirth in her eyes.

"I don't think so," Suzie grinned. "Let's see what else they have," she said as she walked along. The warm breeze coming off the water was enough to soothe her nerves. She was feeling a little anxious about her decision to restore Dune

House. It was a huge undertaking, but she was glad she had Mary to do it with. As she reached the next booth a painting immediately caught her eye. It was large and had a gaudy gold frame, but that wasn't what drew her attention. The painting was of the ocean, only it wasn't perfectly calm. There were white crests on the waves. As she peered at it she noticed that there were faint reflections of the buildings along the beach, including Dune House itself.

"Look, Mary!" she gasped as she looked at the painting more closely. In the reflection of the surface of the water she could see people playing on the beach, as well as many of the buildings that lined the beach itself. It was a beautiful depiction of the heart of the town rather than just the scenery surrounding it. It represented the fun and laid back nature of the environment.

"Wow," Mary said with admiration as she noted the minute details as well. "It's exquisite, I've never seen a painting quite like it," she nodded. Mary glanced up at the man who was running the booth. "Are you the artist?" she asked timidly.

"No," the man shook his head as he looked up from the magazine he was reading. He had a thick mustache like a brush and thinning, glossy black hair that hung a little below the collar of his shirt. He studied Mary's large hat for a surprised moment before he offered them both a mild smile. Suzie thought she recognized him from around town but she couldn't place where. "I'm just selling it," he explained as he set down his magazine which featured fish on the cover. "The artist passed away and these paintings were in her home. There were no heirs so it was relinquished to the town. It's been in storage for some time so now we're selling it off to raise money for a new wing for the library," he tipped his head in Suzie's direction. "Nice to see you again, ma'am," he said with a smile.

Suzie realized where she had met him before. "Oh, it's Luther right? You work with Jason, don't you?" she asked.

"Yes," he said as he stood up from the small stool he was sitting on. His neatly pressed jeans straightened out the moment he stood up. "I've heard about all the hard work you're doing up there at Dune House. I think it's wonderful that you are bringing back such a big part of our town's history."

"Thank you," Suzie replied with a warm smile. "I only hope that I can do it justice," she added modestly.

"You will," Mary said with confidence.

"We will. Starting with this painting," Suzie agreed. "How much is it?" she asked as she looked back up at Luther.

"We're asking fifty dollars for it," he replied with a mild shrug. "Just to be clear, the artist wasn't famous or anything," he added.

"Only fifty?" Suzie asked, and then realized her mistake. "I mean, I'll take it," she laughed. "The artist might not have been famous, but what talent she had."

15

"Yes, she was very talented," Luther agreed with a sad smile. "So young, too, and so tragic the way her life ended."

"Tragic?" Mary asked as Suzie pulled out her wallet and paid for the painting. Luther handed Suzie her change along with a receipt for her purchase.

"Yes. I don't know the whole story but it seems she jumped into the ocean," he sighed as he gazed at the painting. "Makes you wonder what was going through her mind, that she could see so much beauty, but it wasn't enough for her to want to live."

"So true," Mary nodded as she looked back at the painting with a new perspective. "It seems like she loved this town."

"She would have. She grew up here," he smiled a bit more. "She always loved to paint, was in the art festival every year," his voice trailed off for a moment as his smile faded. "This is the only painting she had left in her home."

16

"I think it will be perfect for Dune House," Suzie said with confidence as Luther carefully wrapped the painting in brown paper to protect it.

"Would you like me to take it to your car?" he offered as he looked back up at Suzie. His light brown eyes seemed to light up a little when he looked at her. "Perhaps I could help you hang it?" he suggested.

"No, thank you," Suzie said politely. "I think Mary and I can manage."

"Oh, okay," he nodded and managed a smile. "Thanks for your purchase."

"You're very welcome, and thanks for the painting," Suzie grinned.

Mary took one side of the painting and Suzie took the other. The two made their way carefully back to the parking lot. Mary huffed a little as she carried the painting. It was a bit heavier than it looked, and it looked quite heavy to begin with.

"And why did you turn down that fine gentleman's offer?" Mary asked through heavy breaths. "This frame weighs a ton!"

"I didn't really think it would be this heavy," Suzie admitted as she grunted and did her best to keep her side of the painting even with Mary's. Mary had always been the stronger of the pair.

"He would have been happy to do it, too," Mary pointed out with annoyance. "He had eyes for you."

"Oh please," Suzie shook her head as they finally made it to the car. She let her side of the painting down carefully, then Mary dropped hers down as well.

"What? He was handsome, and kind," Mary pointed out her voice a little reproachful. "What's so wrong with that? Weren't you the one just talking about the empty chair?" she reminded her friend.

"Nothing's wrong with it," Suzie admitted as she opened the back door so they could slide the painting in the back seat. "It's just that, well," she cleared her throat.

"Perhaps you have eyes for a certain captain?" Mary suggested with a smile.

"Mary!" Suzie said with exasperation. "Be careful what you say, small towns have big ears," she glanced around to be sure that no one was close enough to have overheard.

"And what's so wrong if everyone knows?" Mary asked as she helped Suzie guide the painting into the car. "It isn't as if he doesn't have eyes for you, too," Mary suppressed a laugh.

"Look Mary, I have a lot on my mind with the B & B, and..." Suzie began to say but Mary cut her off before she could continue to make excuses.

"And, you're a little afraid you might like him a little too much?" Mary suggested as she closed the back door of the car.

Suzie pursed her lips and fixed her friend with an annoyed glare. Mary always had a way of knowing everything that was going on in Suzie's mind, no matter how hard she tried to hide it.

"I just don't know if I want to like him, or him

to like me," Suzie pointed out and shook her head. "Paul's a very nice man, but that doesn't mean that there should be anything between us," Suzie bit into her bottom lip and frowned. "I mean we've only bumped into each other a few times. We haven't even been on a date."

"Well, you should," Mary said with a sheepish smile.

"There's nothing wrong with taking things slow."

"No, not at all," Mary agreed innocently as she opened the passenger door. Suzie walked around to the driver's side. Mary met her eyes over the top of the car. "Slow and sensual," Mary added with a light wink and a faint growl.

"Mary!" Suzie gasped but Mary had already ducked inside the car. By the time Suzie started the car they were both laughing. The truth was Paul was on Suzie's mind, quite often. A little too often. She had never let a man distract her from her work, but sometimes when she looked out

20

over the water, and thought of Paul out there somewhere on his boat, she yearned to join him.

As Suzie drove back to Dune House, she had another person on her mind, the artist of the painting.

"I wonder what could drive a young woman to take her own life?" Suzie asked out loud as Mary gave up on finding any music she liked and turned off the radio.

"Romance," Mary said with a sage nod. "I am certain it was romance."

"Do you really think so?" Suzie asked and frowned. "What man could be worth that?"

"It's not so much the man," Mary said quietly. "It's more the moments."

"What do you mean by that?" Suzie asked curiously.

"When you share certain moments with a person, those moments will always belong to both of you. My husband was there for the births of both of my children. I can't have that memory alone, to myself. It belongs to him, too. When that person you share such a special moment with, breaks your heart, you don't just grieve the man, you grieve the moment."

Suzie smiled sympathetically at Mary as she pulled into the driveway of Dune House.

"I'm sorry, Mary, I know that you are going through so much," she murmured.

"Actually," Mary managed a smile. "I'm just starting to feel free again. And I have to admit, it's a nice feeling."

"I'm glad," Suzie said as she turned the car off and leaned over to hug her friend. "Just remember, the best part of life is that there are always more moments."

"I guess," Mary laughed. "I'm pretty sure I know what my next few moments have in store for me. We better get this painting inside before I decide that I'd rather take a nap."

"Good idea," Suzie agreed.

Chapter Two

Suzie and Mary managed to get the painting up the hill and into the house before they laid it on the floor.

"Wow, that was a work out," Suzie groaned as she wiped sweat off her forehead.

"It was worth it, though," Mary said as she tore away some of the brown paper. "It's as perfect as you said it would be."

Suzie stared at the painting after they had unwrapped it. She studied it for a few minutes, before she shifted her weight from one foot to the other. She placed one hand on her hip and tilted her head slightly to the side.

"Well, it is a very nice painting," she said slowly.

Mary looked up at her incredulously. "Suzie? What are you saying?" she demanded.

Suzie tapped a fingertip against her bottom

lip as she looked down at the painting and then up at the wall. "I'm not so sure it fits…" she began to say.

"Oh no!" Mary said as she stood up straight so quickly that she had to reach behind her and lightly massage her lower back. "We just hauled that thing up here. It's staying. It's going on that wall!"

"But Mary," Suzie shook her head. "Something isn't quite right."

"What could not be right?" Mary asked with growing exasperation. She was usually incredibly patient, but it was clear that her patience was running thin. "You asked for the perfect painting, and we found it. It's nothing short of a miracle!"

Suzie lifted her eyes to Mary's. She quirked a brow slightly. "A miracle in a hideous gold frame," she pointed out.

"Oh no…" Mary began, about to lecture her again and then looked down at the frame. "Oh well," she sighed as she stared at the frame. "I guess you have a point about that."

"See?" Suzie said and crouched down in front of the painting. "The color is just going to clash with everything."

"Okay, okay, but wait," Mary said as she paced back and forth. "We don't have to throw the painting out with the frame, if you know what I mean. We can always replace the frame with a different one."

Suzie was perfectly still as she thought about this. Then suddenly she stood straight up.

"Mary, you're a genius!" she said gleefully. "We can get the perfect frame for it no problem!"

"What about this one?" Mary pointed to the painting that was still leaning against the wall. "It looks like it's the same size, and it looked nice on the wall."

"That's true," Suzie agreed as she glanced between the two paintings swiftly. "Yes, I think that could work! Help me get it onto the big table," she requested. Together they guided the painting onto the big dining room table.

Suzie carefully released the painting from the frame. She expected she might tear it a little, but it came free surprisingly easily. "I think this is going to work," she said happily.

"It seems like the painting has been in this frame quite long," Suzie murmured as she lifted the painting carefully out of the frame. "I wonder how long ago the artist passed?"

She was studying the painting intently, waiting for a response from Mary. When she didn't hear one, she glanced up at Mary. "Mary?" she asked. "What do you think?"

"I think we should figure out what that is," Mary replied in a whisper as she pointed at the frame.

"Huh?" Suzie glanced down at the frame and her eyes widened. She nearly dropped the painting she was holding. Inside the frame, previously hidden behind the painting was a hand drawn map. It was designed just like a treasure map, with symbols and dashes to represent locations and movements. Suzie's heart began to race as she stared down at the map.

"Do you think it's real?" she asked when she looked up at Mary.

"Well I," Mary reached up and brushed her hair back from her eyes as she frowned. "I don't know. I mean, are treasure maps ever real? It looks similar to the ones I used to make for the kids at their birthday parties."

"It could be real," Suzie said in a murmur and ran a fingertip along the edge of the map. It lifted easily from the frame. "Why else would she go to all the trouble of hiding it?" she wondered aloud.

"I don't know," Mary said as she stepped closer to take a look. "Maybe it was just a sentimental thing. I mean, this was the only painting they found of hers."

"That's true," Suzie nodded with a hint of disappointment. "I used to love watching the kids go on those treasure hunts," she mentioned quietly.

"Watching?" Mary laughed and shook her head. "You used to try to beat them to the treasure!"

Suzie smiled guiltily and locked eyes with Mary briefly as a flood of affection rushed through her. She had never wanted children of her own, but she had enjoyed being part of Mary's children's lives. Mary had always made sure she was involved if she wanted to be. It was one of those moments when she reflected on just how deeply Mary's husband had betrayed her. She was a fantastic mother, and a wonderful wife, but no matter what happened in her life, she had never stopped being an amazing friend to Suzie.

"So, what do you think?" Suzie asked with a glimmer of mischief in her eyes.

"Think about what?" Mary asked in return as she narrowed her eyes. "The painting? I think it will be perfect."

"No, the map," Suzie said with a roll of her

eyes.

"What about it?" Mary asked with a look of confusion.

"Don't you think we should see where it leads?" Suzie pressed impatiently.

"Well, I'm sure it's just some kind of prank," Mary said with a shake of her head. "Does anyone really make treasure maps anymore? Do you think a pirate drew this?" she laughed a little.

"Mary!" Suzie said with some frustration. "Be serious for just a moment. Why would someone go to the trouble of hiding this if there wasn't something to be found by following it?"

"It could be sentimental," Mary pointed out with lingering hesitation.

"It could be," Suzie agreed. "But, even if it is, I'd like to discover that kind of treasure, too. Maybe it leads to a secret spring in the woods, or a tree with special carvings. What could it hurt to try to find out?"

Mary nodded as she smiled mischievously. "I

29

think you're right, it would be a lot of fun. Plus we'd get to know the area a bit more."

"Now, you're thinking my way," Suzie grinned. She lifted the map carefully out of the frame. "I'd guess that it is the same artist who drew this map," she said thoughtfully. "It looks like it was done by a similar hand."

"Well, that makes sense," Mary nodded as she peered at the map as well. "But it doesn't make much sense."

Suzie laid the map out on the table beside the frame. Maybe it wasn't even a map of an area around Garber. But there was no harm in trying to work out where it led, even if it amounted to nothing. Suzie studied the map a moment longer, very intrigued by the symbols included on it. But she knew that if she got engrossed in it right away she was going to lose track of getting the painting up on the wall.

"Well, I suppose it's a mystery that will have to wait," she said with some disappointment. "We need to get that painting in the other frame and hung up before anything can damage it."

"Yes, and we're losing natural light," Mary said as she tipped her head towards the floor to ceiling windows. Dark clouds had begun rolling in along the water. It gave the splashing waves a desolate look. Suzie felt a twinge of sorrow as she wondered if the sea had looked this way the day that the artist of the painting had plunged into it. It was unsettling to think that such a beautiful sight could turn into something quite deadly.

"Yes, you're right, I'm never going to be certain if I don't see it in natural light."

"Do you think we can use the same holes since we're using the same frame?" Mary asked hopefully as she squinted at the wall.

"It should be fine," Suzie nodded as she locked the painting into the frame from the first painting. "Wow, you were right, Mary this looks so much better," she sighed as she studied the painting.

"And it will be much lighter," Mary laughed.

"Do you think that there's anything hidden in the painting itself?" Suzie wondered as she gazed at it with a deep appreciation.

"I think there are many things hidden in that painting," Mary said softly as she studied all the faint faces that were barely visible etched into the water. She then climbed onto the stepladder.

"Secrets that the artist took to her grave, I'm sure," Suzie said as she helped Mary hoist it up onto the wall while trying to keep the stepladder as steady as possible. Her words were punctuated by a sharp clap of thunder. Suzie and Mary both gasped with surprise, even though they had been expecting the storm. Before they could even comment on the loud rumbling, there was a knock on the door.

"Knock, knock," a familiar voice called out as the door of Dune House swung slowly open. Suzie looked up with surprise and then smiled warmly as Paul stepped through the door.

"I hope I'm not interrupting," he said as he stepped forward quickly to help with the hanging of the painting. Suzie's heart fluttered faintly when Paul's hands brushed over hers to help grasp the frame of the painting. Once it was in place, he let his hands fall back to his sides, and they brushed past Suzie's hands once more. She quickly turned away to hide the heat she felt rising in her cheeks.

"Thanks Paul," Mary said as she made her way down the ladder. "Well Suzie, what's the verdict?" Mary asked as she took a few steps back to look at the painting.

"It's hard to tell in this light," Suzie said hesitantly. "But I couldn't imagine a more perfect painting."

"It is beautiful," Paul said as he also took in the sight of the painting. "Had I known it was for sale I might have snatched it up myself."

"Did you know the artist?" Suzie asked quickly.

"No, I'm afraid not," he shook his head. "I don't spend a lot of time in town. I'm usually on my boat. Otherwise, I tend to keep to myself," he added.

Suzie was slightly intrigued by his revelation. She hadn't considered that he might be a loner. He seemed so friendly and warm natured. But perhaps that was only when he was around her.

"Some storm coming in," Mary mentioned as she glanced out the window at the brooding sky.

"Yes, that's why I stopped by," Paul said in a distant voice as if he was waking from a dream. "I wanted to make sure that you two had everything you needed in case you lose power."

"I think we're equipped," Suzie said with a smile. "But thank you for checking on us."

"These summer storms can be fierce," Paul added his serious tone returning. "This one should pass by tomorrow afternoon, but I wanted to be sure you didn't need help with anything."

"I appreciate that," Suzie said softly, and then

added quickly. "I mean, we both do." Mary was still staring out at the rough waves. She was hugging herself as she stared.

"Mary? Are you okay?" Suzie asked.

"Sorry, I had almost forgotten how frightening the water can be," she murmured.

"In this weather it can be," Paul agreed. "I'll be bunking on land tonight."

"Well, we have some rooms free," Mary suggested innocently. Suzie sent her a withering glare when Paul was looking out over the water.

"Thanks, but I have my regular place," he said mildly.

Suzie's chest tightened at that comment. She wondered if he was talking about a girlfriend's place. She hadn't even really considered that he might already be with someone. But then she told herself to stop being silly as he was probably referring to the motel where they met each other the first time when Suzie had just moved to town.

"We found something inside the frame of the

painting," she said abruptly. She was a little surprised that she had mentioned it. She hadn't really intended to tell Paul, but once she had she thought it was a great idea. He would know the water and the beaches better than anyone else.

"What did you find?" he asked curiously.

"It's over there," Mary gestured to the dining room table. He walked over with Suzie to take a look at the map.

"Wow," he said with wide eyes. "This is some piece of art," he breathed out. "Reminds me of playing with friends when I was a boy. We would hide treasure and draw maps in the sand for our friends to follow."

"Well, then you should be an expert," Suzie said with a warm smile. "Just what we need, to find where it leads."

"Really?" he asked and looked right into Suzie's eyes. Suzie was startled by the sudden connection but relaxed the moment his lips spread into a smile of excitement. "I can't wait!"

he announced. He looked back down at the map and then tapped his finger lightly against one of the images on the map. "I think I might actually know where this is," he added in a murmur. "It looks like a place very few people know about."

"Are you sure?" Suzie asked with excitement.

"I can't be positive," he said with a slight shake of his head. "But, from these symbols," he pointed to the open water depicted in the map, followed by three piles of rocks and a thin stream of water. "From what this shows, it looks like a little inlet that even a boat can't get near."

"How amazing that you might know where it is," Mary said happily.

"I could take you both out to find it?" he offered as he looked between the two women. "That is, if you don't mind sharing your treasure hunt."

"That would be wonderful," Suzie said with a wide grin.

"Unfortunately, with the weather this bad, I

won't be able to take you until it clears," Paul said. "It wouldn't be safe."

"That does not sound like fun," Mary said with a grimace.

"Mary's a little nervous about boats," Suzie confided in Paul.

"Oh well, that's all right," he smiled as he looked over at Mary. "I promise not to let you fall off."

"That is not very reassuring," Mary said with a short laugh.

Their amusement was silenced by another strong roll of thunder.

"Well, I better get going," Paul said as he nodded to Mary and smiled at Suzie. "I'll give you a call tomorrow afternoon if the weather is clear. Is that okay with you?"

"That's great," Suzie nodded. "And thanks again for checking in."

"If you two run into any trouble, just give me

a ring," Paul said as he walked out the door. The rain had just begun pelting down.

"Are you sure you'll be safe to drive in this?" Suzie asked hesitantly as she looked up at the gathering clouds.

"I'll be fine," Paul murmured and held her gaze as she looked into his eyes. The moment drew out longer than it should have, before Suzie lowered her eyes.

"Have a good night, Paul," she said cheerfully and backed away.

His smile didn't falter as he turned and walked towards his car.

Suzie was stealing a glance at him walking away when she felt a sharp smack along the back of her head. It wasn't enough to cause much pain, but it certainly startled her.

"What are you thinking?" Mary demanded as Suzie spun around to face her.

"That my head hurts," Suzie complained with narrowed eyes and rubbed at the back of her head.

"He came here to check on you, and offered to ferry you around the neighborhood, and then gave you the 'kiss me now' look!" Mary huffed as Suzie closed the door.

"The what look?" Suzie laughed and shook her head. "Mary, have you been reading some kind of romance novel?"

"I know that look," Mary said sternly. "Just because I was married for so long, doesn't mean I don't have good instincts. Paul was lingering because he hoped for a kiss, and you backed off! Why?" Mary met her friend's eyes, and Suzie realized she wasn't as angry as she was concerned.

"I don't know," Suzie shrugged slightly. "I've made it this far on my own, I guess." Even though Suzie had had her share of male interest over the years she had never really had anyone very serious.

"Trust me, Suzie," Mary said with a slight sigh. "It's much better to have someone checking to see if you're safe."

"Maybe," Suzie frowned. "But what happens when you get used to that? What happens when it gets taken away?"

"Oh," Mary nodded a little. "I suppose you have a point there."

"See, no more smacking," Suzie admonished as she walked back over to the map.

"I still say you're avoiding," Mary warned as she stepped up beside her.

"Nothing to avoid," Suzie insisted. "Maybe the key to finding out more about this map, is finding out more about the artist," Suzie suggested thoughtfully as she continued to study the map.

"Well, I imagine if her death was so tragic there would be a record of it in the local newspaper," Mary suggested.

"I bet there is," Suzie nodded. "Good thing we know of a friendly librarian, hmm?"

"I don't know if friendly is the right word," Mary laughed a little. "But I'm sure that Louis would help us out."

"We're not going anywhere tonight," Suzie said with disappointment as the wind whipped by the window.

"No, but we can try to head out first thing in the morning," Mary yawned. "I'm a little worn out from toting that painting around."

"Me, too," Suzie agreed. As they walked down the hall towards the kitchen, Suzie felt that strange uneasy feeling once more. She glanced towards the floor-to-ceiling windows that lined the kitchen. It was too dark to see clearly but for a split-second she thought for sure that someone was standing outside, looking in.

"Mary," Suzie gasped as she grabbed Mary's arm. "Do you see that?"

"What?" Mary asked as she peered at the window. "I don't see anything there," she yawned again.

When Suzie looked again, she didn't see anything either. "I guess it is nothing," she sighed. "Let's have something to eat and then an early night. We need to get some good rest. We hunt for treasure tomorrow!"

Chapter Three

The next morning, Suzie woke up with the memory of the face in the window on her mind. She was still feeling uneasy about it. The storm had died down to a steady rain with an occasional gust of wind. When Suzie paused beside Mary's room she could hear her light snoring. Suzie grabbed her jacket and her boots and threw them on over her pajamas. She didn't want to wait any longer to check on what she thought she had seen the night before.

As Suzie opened the door to step outside she felt a rush of cool air. It felt almost icy compared to the balmy beach weather she had become used to. She tightened her jacket around her neck and walked around the side of the large house. When she neared the kitchen she studied the sand for any sign of footprints. But the way the rain was pelting down made it clear that any evidence from the night before had likely been washed away. As she stepped closer to the window she noticed something. Small smudges on the glass. She was very careful to clean the windows, and knew that neither she nor Mary had touched the glass since it was cleaned. She frowned as she studied them. They were nothing more than nearly invisible blemishes. It would be hard for anyone to take them as evidence of someone looking in from outside. But Suzie just couldn't shake the certainty that someone had been there the night before.

When she felt a hand touch her shoulder, Suzie nearly jumped out of her skin.

"Ah!" she cried out as she spun to face whoever was touching her. "I have mace!" she shouted with her eyes half-closed.

"You have pajamas," Mary pointed out and tried not to laugh. "I'm sorry if I scared you. I thought you heard me coming."

"Oh Mary, you nearly gave me a heart attack," Suzie sighed and laid her hand against her chest.

"Well honestly, I thought you might be sleep-walking. I saw you out here through the kitchen windows and you were staring so blankly at the glass that I thought maybe you had wandered out," Mary frowned and studied Suzie intently. "Why exactly are you standing out here in the rain in your pajamas?"

Suzie didn't want to frighten her friend so she didn't tell Mary about the fingerprints and the face she had seen, especially when she had no proof that anything had really happened.

"Just wanted some fresh air," Suzie said softly.

Mary narrowed her eyes as if she did not believe her, but she did not press.

"Well, come inside before you get sick," Mary insisted and tugged at her friend's arm.

"First you try to give me a heart attack, and now you're concerned about my health?" Suzie joked to break the tension.

"I didn't mean to," Mary insisted. "Let's get

some breakfast. I think that the weather is mild enough for us to head to the library, don't you?"

"Have you been dreaming about treasure maps?" Suzie asked as they stepped back into Dune House.

"Maybe," Mary replied with a short laugh. "I'll get some breakfast going for us, you go get dried off and dressed."

As Suzie changed, her mind traveled back to the fingerprints on the window. Was it possible that someone really had been outside the night before? If so, who could it be? She was still feeling unsettled as she had breakfast with Mary. She tried to distract herself with talk of looking for where the map might lead them.

"What do you think it could be?" Suzie asked as she took the last bite of her eggs.

"I just hope it's nothing too sad," Mary said with a frown. "She did kill herself after all, maybe the map leads to some of the reasons why."

"Maybe, I hadn't thought of that," Suzie said

in a murmur. "It could be something like a final confession."

"Well, the best way to find out is to ask," Mary said as she cleared the breakfast dishes. Suzie washed and dried them while Mary was getting ready to go. Suzie noticed as they left Dune House that Mary had applied a modest amount of pale pink lipstick. She smiled a little to herself as she realized her friend was beginning to experiment with her looks again. To Suzie that meant that she was beginning to come out of the painful fog of her divorce. As they drove to the library the wind was still whipping wildly. It didn't affect the roads much, but the waves were large and intimidating as they crashed against the shore.

"Good thing Paul's on land," she muttered to herself as she turned down the main street towards the library. There was no sign of the art fair that had taken place the day before.

"I'm still so nervous about going out on the water with him," Mary sighed and shook her head. "I know I shouldn't be, but I remember what it was like to be out in the middle of the water on that awful cruise ship. It just seems like there's no way to get back to land. It makes me a little scared."

"Try not to worry too much, Paul won't take us out on the water unless it's safe," Suzie assured her as she parked the car in the library's parking lot.

"Look at you, already trusting," Mary said with a playful smile as she stepped out of the car. Suzie stepped out as well and shook her head as they walked towards the library.

"Stop it, Mary, it's not going to happen," she said firmly.

"Sure," Mary nodded as she opened the door for Suzie and they escaped the rain that was coming down a little harder.

When they walked into the library, their footsteps muffled by thick carpet, Suzie spotted Louis who was busy with a sticky-fingered toddler. The child seemed to think that a book about ice cream was for licking, not reading.

"Ugh," Suzie cringed and looked away from the sight.

"Isn't he adorable?" Mary cooed as she watched the child slobber all over the book.

"If you say so," Suzie laughed and began looking over the books on the sale table. As she was sorting through them she had a strange feeling. She couldn't quite place what it was, but she just felt uneasy. She looked up and glanced over her shoulder. Yet again it felt as if someone might be watching her. Shaking off the sensation she turned back to the books on the table. There wasn't anything of much interest to her, so when Mary called to her she headed over without hesitation.

"Look at this," she said as she handed her a thin book.

"What is it?" Suzie asked as she glanced over the images on the cover. It was more like a booklet than a book.

"It showcases all the local artists in Garber and the nearby towns," Mary explained. "Turn to the first page."

When Suzie opened the book she found a similar painting to the one she had purchased, pictured on the glossy page. The artist's name was printed underneath the picture.

"Alexandria Black," Suzie read in a soft tone. "I wonder if there's a picture," she flipped to the back of the booklet where there were a few small black and white photographs of the artists. She found Alexandria's name and was surprised by the picture beside it. The young woman in the picture was smiling warmly. She had hair that flowed down over her shoulders in luxurious waves. Her soft features were very pretty, and her expression was eager, without a hint to what the future would hold for her.

"Oh Mary, look how young she was," Suzie said with a shocked gasp.

"She couldn't be much older than my

daughter," Mary said with a frown. "I couldn't imagine feeling so desolate at such a young age."

Alexandria was smiling right into the camera, and Suzie could detect pride in her eyes. She might have just been in her twenties. She appeared so full of life it was hard to believe that she was no longer living.

"Hello Mary, Suzie," Louis nodded at both women as he walked up to them. "Sorry for the wait," he pushed his glasses up along his nose and peered at the book Suzie was holding. "Are you still looking for some art for Dune House?" he asked curiously.

"Actually, I found the perfect painting," Suzie admitted as she held the book out to him. "But now I'm curious about the artist of the painting. Do you know anything about Alexandria Black?" she asked.

"Oh," a dark expression consumed Louis' otherwise plain features. His brown eyebrows knitted and he looked from the picture of

Alexandria then up at Suzie with hesitation. "Yes, I do know a few things about her," he said softly.

"Are you okay, Louis?" Mary asked with concern as his voice trembled slightly when he spoke.

"I'm sorry," he forced a smile on his lips. "It's just she was a friend of mine."

"She was?" Suzie asked with surprise and then realized what that meant. "Oh Louis, I'm sorry for your loss."

"Oh, it was some time ago," he shrugged a little. "Maybe ten years," he added and then briefly closed his eyes. "I was quite good friends with her late father. When we were younger we used to go fishing together and he often used to bring his young daughter with," he said with a faraway look. "He died quite young. She and I weren't terribly close, but when someone you know does something like that, it is hard to get passed," he shook his head as if he was still in disbelief about it.

"So, she did commit suicide?" Suzie asked as gently as she could. It was a very sensitive topic to broach.

"Yes," he sighed as he glanced towards the front window of the library. "She jumped off a cliff, not far from Dune House actually," he cleared his throat. "It was a shock for the whole town. She was well-known for her artwork and she was very generous with it. She would donate it to the local museums and even here to the library. Well that is, until she sold it all off."

"Was she struggling with depression?" Mary asked tentatively.

"That's the thing," Louis said with a shake of his head. "She was never depressed, at least not that I saw. I mean I know that people can hide these things, but she was the last person I would expect to be depressed. She was always so warm, and had a kind thing to say about everyone she met. Even that screw-up she married."

"Screw-up?" Suzie pressed curiously, it was

the first she had heard of a husband. "She looks so young to have been married," she added.

"She married him at eighteen. Thought she was in love. I tried to warn her, a few of her friends did. Darren was from a few towns over, I forget which one now. He wasn't a bad guy, but he was always getting into bad situations. She was always defending him and was always supporting him. They seemed so in love. But, he was determined he was going to be rich, and would try just about anything to make that happen. Not long before she passed away he was arrested, and I guess with him being in prison, it might have sent her into a deep depression that no one noticed," Louis shrugged slightly. "She sold all of her paintings but one, and most of her belongings to try to get him out of prison, but there was nothing anyone could do. It's the only thing that makes any sense. Who can know what's really going on in someone's mind, right?"

"Right," Mary agreed gently. Suzie was staring down at the photograph of Alexandria. It was hard to believe that such a youthful smile could be hiding all of the difficulties she had faced.

"So sad to see such a talent wasted," she said with a sigh.

"Yes, it was. She was so desperate to help him. She became obsessed with trying to get him released. No one understood, because it was clear he was guilty, he never even tried to claim he was innocent," he frowned. "Once all of her artwork was gone she had nothing left to sell. Maybe she just gave up."

"What was so special about the one she kept, do you know?" Mary asked as she looked intently at Louis. "We bought one of her paintings yesterday, it must be the one she held onto as it was part of her estate."

"Oh?" Louis asked with surprise. "Well, they must have got around to clearing out some storage. I know she always had her favorite. She wouldn't ever really tell me why it was her favorite, but after Darren was arrested I would always find her sitting and staring at it when I dropped by to check on her."

Suzie's eyes widened slightly. She wondered if the painting was never sold because Alexandria knew the map was hidden inside the frame. If that was the case then the map had obviously been important to her, which might mean it could lead to something valuable after all.

"Are there any articles about her death, or her husband's arrest?" Suzie asked hopefully.

"I'm sure there's something. I'll bring up the dates for you," he said and headed back to his desk. "Is there a reason you're so interested?" he asked.

"I just think the painting is beautiful," Suzie said with a faint smile. "It might seem silly but it seemed as if I was guided to it. I'd like to know as much as I can about the artist who could create something so stunning."

"Yes, she had a way of capturing nature,"

Louis agreed and printed out a list of pages. "Here are the pages and dates of the newspapers that mention Alexandria's name, or Darren's. Let me know if you need any help with the microfilm," he added.

"Thanks, Louis," Mary said as she took the paper. "And I'm sorry for your loss."

"Thank you," Louis said with a slight smile. "It's been some time since I thought of Alexandria. It's nice to remember the good memories."

Suzie and Mary walked to the back of the library where the machine was located.

Suzie sat down in front of the screen and Mary pulled up a chair beside her. They began perusing the articles for the dates that Louis had mentioned.

"Look, there," Mary said as she pointed to a small article almost hidden by large ads. "Local artist meets a tragic end," she read the title of the article.

Suzie zoomed into the article and looked at the picture of the artist.

"Alexandria Black was found today at the bottom of Alba's Cliff," she read in a whisper. "It's believed that she committed suicide. No further information is available at this time."

"It doesn't say much, does it?" Mary said with a sigh. "It's sad to think that her life could be summed up in so few words. Didn't she have any family?"

"It doesn't list anything about family," Suzie said with a frown. "It seems that perhaps she only had her husband after her father died. Imagine how he must have felt getting news like that while being locked up?"

Mary shook her head. "This whole thing is just too sad."

"It is sad," Suzie agreed. "But it's also intriguing. The article doesn't mention her husband, but Louis said there might be articles about the day he was arrested. I wonder what he's in for?"

"Let's take a look," Mary replied. Suzie flipped through the articles until she came to the date that Louis had given them. Splashed across the front page of the newspaper was an article about three men getting arrested for armed robbery.

"Wow," Mary said as she read the title of the article. "Three men arrested for armed robbery," she shook her head. "That's more than getting in a little bit of trouble."

"It says that Darren Black was one of the three men who robbed Washington Bank. They were caught two days later, and arrested, but the money was never recovered," Suzie said with a light cluck of her tongue. "Darren got himself into some serious trouble."

"Do you think he's still in prison?" Mary wondered out loud.

"I think he would be with that charge," Suzie replied as she flipped through the articles. "We should visit the prison and see what he has to say about this painting."

"The prison?" Mary asked with wide eyes. "I'm not sure I'd want to go there."

"Well, it looks like if we want to visit Darren Black we're going to have to head to the local cemetery instead," Suzie said as her eyes fell on another article related to Darren.

"Is he dead?" Mary asked as she read over the article as well.

"He was killed during a prison riot," Suzie said softly. "Not more than a year after Alexandria died."

"Incredible," Mary shook her head. "I guess we've reached a dead end then," she said with some disappointment. "With Alexandria gone, and Darren gone, there's no one to give us any more insight into that map."

Suzie sat back in her chair. Her eyes were narrowed and her lips pursed.

"Uh oh, what are you brewing in that mind of yours?" Mary asked suspiciously as she recognized the expression.

"I'm just thinking," Suzie said innocently.

"About what?" Mary pressed.

"Well, the stolen money was never recovered. But all three men who stole it were arrested," Suzie pointed out.

"And?" Mary asked.

"And, it's likely they stashed the money somewhere, right?" Suzie asked, her eyes lighting up.

"You think the map leads to the stolen money?" Mary asked with wide eyes. "You think Alexandria knew about it?"

"Think about it," Suzie nodded. "She and Darren were head over heels in love, they only had each other. If Darren did something as wild as rob a bank, who do you think he would trust the money with or at the very least the location of the money?"

"But, if Alexandria knew where the money

was, why would she jump off a cliff?" Mary asked. "She could have been a very rich woman. She would have had more than enough to set up a beautiful life for herself and Darren when he got out. Do you think she did it out of guilt?"

"I would think if she was feeling guilty she would have just turned the money in," Suzie said thoughtfully. "What would drive her to jump?"

"Maybe the secret was too much pressure," Mary suggested in a whisper.

"Or maybe, she didn't jump at all," Suzie said with a raised eyebrow.

"What are you saying, Suzie?" Mary asked with a gasp and then lowered her voice. "Do you think Alexandria was murdered?"

"I think we need to find out more about all of this," Suzie said sternly.

"But how?" Mary asked. "It doesn't sound like any of Alexandria's friends knew what was happening in her life. With Darren gone, there's no one else to ask."

"Maybe not," Suzie said and shook her head. "But I'm not willing to let go of this little mystery yet."

Just as she spoke her cell phone began to ring shrilly. She answered it quickly and ducked her head to avoid the admonishing glances from other people at the library.

"Hello?" she asked.

"Hi Suzie, it's me Paul," Paul said nervously.

"Hi Paul," Suzie instantly smiled, and then forced her expression to be more casual when she saw Mary eying her suspiciously.

"Listen, I know I promised to take you and Mary out on the water today, but it's still pretty choppy out there. I think we're better off waiting until tomorrow afternoon. Is that all right with you?"

"Of course it is," Suzie replied though she couldn't hide a twinge of disappointment. "No point in treasure hunting if we're going to end up stranded instead."

"I wouldn't let that happen," Paul promised her. "But from the weather report the sea is going to be pretty wild for most of the night tonight, it's best to wait until it's calm."

"Thanks Paul," Suzie said quickly. "I'm looking forward to it, any time we can go."

"Me too," Paul admitted. "Did you weather the storm okay?" he asked.

"We were fine," Suzie promised him.

"Let's plan for two in the afternoon tomorrow, okay?" he suggested.

"Sounds great, thanks again," Suzie said before hanging up the phone. "Looks like we're stuck on dry land today," Suzie said with a sigh as she looked at Mary.

"Like you said, Paul is cautious," Mary smiled.

"Well, he did say the weather is going to get a little wild this evening, so maybe we should head back. There are some things I can get done around the house while we wait out this storm," Suzie suggested. As they left the library Louis waved to them.

Chapter Four

When Suzie and Mary arrived back at Dune House it was hard for Suzie to focus on the tasks at hand. She wanted more than anything to know what had happened to Alexandria, and where the map led. Mary was rummaging around in the kitchen when she suddenly laughed.

"All this running in and out of town and we're completely out of bread, cereal and coffee," she groaned. "I can't believe I forgot to pick some up."

"We'll go back and grab it," Suzie said as she picked up the car keys.

"That's all right, I'll go," Mary said. "I know you have things you want to do here. Plus, there were a few books at the library I was interested in. I got distracted when we began looking at the microfilm. I'll be back in just a little while."

Suzie sensed that Mary might want some time alone, so she didn't push it. "Just be careful of the weather," Suzie said as she dropped the keys into her hand.

"I will be," Mary promised her. "No finding any treasure while I'm gone, please!" she called back over her shoulder as she headed out the door.

Suzie smiled as she watched her friend leave. She knew that Mary was still dealing with the emotions of her divorce, and some of what she was experiencing was impossible for Suzie to understand. She had never had her heart broken, and she hoped she never would.

As she began folding the linens she had recently washed that would go in the rooms that she was finished decorating, her mind drifted back to Alexandria. She imagined the young woman, so in love, and what it must have been like for her if Darren left the money with her. Alexandria had probably been terrified, and then crushed when Darren was arrested. Justice was served, but Alexandria had been permanently wounded in the process. Still, Suzie found it hard to believe that she could have jumped off the cliff.

She finished folding the linens and pulled on some rubber gloves to continue working on one of the bathrooms that needed a lot of attention.

"Hello?" a rough voice called out. Suzie tensed as she heard the door bang against the outside wall. Someone had swung it open very hard. She pulled off her gloves and walked towards the front door very cautiously.

"Hello?" she replied as she took note of the two men standing just inside the door. One was tall and very thick, as broad as any bear she had seen. His hair was disheveled half-splayed across his forehead and hanging in his eyes, something between brown and black. He was glowering at her in a way that made her very uneasy. The man beside him was just as tall but was as thin as a pole. His eyes were dark and narrowed as they settled on Suzie. For a brief moment she thought she knew them from somewhere, but the moment passed as the thin man began to speak.

"We're looking for a room," he said gruffly and took a step further into the house without being invited. "This looks like a good place," he added, though his voice did not indicate a compliment.

"Oh, I'm very sorry but we're not open for business yet," Suzie replied her heart starting to beat faster. Something about the two men made her think she was in danger. She wasn't sure if it was their manner of dress which was sloppy at best, or the fact that neither had managed even the slightest smile or warmth in their tone. She glanced nervously over her shoulder, well aware that she was alone in Dune House. Then she looked back at the two men, hoping they would take the hint and leave.

"I'm sure you've got a bed we can sleep in," the thin man said and reached up to adjust the baseball cap he was wearing. It had no image on it, just a solid black cap. "We don't need much, just a roof over our heads. Would you deny us that?" he asked in a polite tone, but his eyes remained just as cold.

"Again, I'm very sorry," Suzie said quickly,

she didn't want word to get around that she wasn't welcoming to guests. "But we can't host any guests until Dune House is officially open, it's an insurance issue," she explained with a slight shrug.

"Sure, insurance," the bear-sized man muttered with a shake of his head. Suzie was startled when he spoke as he had been staring at her with a sneer in silence for quite some time. "We're not going to report anything to any insurance. Are we Al?" he asked the thin man.

"That may be true," Suzie said cordially, she was becoming more and more anxious with the two of them blocking the door. "But, I can't take that kind of risk. I'm sure you understand. There is a fine motel a mile or so down the beach. I'm sure they will have a room available."

"Hmm, I get the point," the tall, thin man, Al, nodded. "Let's go George, we're not wanted here."

Suzie felt some relief as she watched the two men turn to leave. But George stopped and turned back to look at her.

"Do you have a restroom I could use?" he asked, his hard eyes boring into her, his broad shoulders tense and his muscles flexed. She was well aware she would not be capable of defending herself against a man his size.

Suzie was normally one to be welcoming and accommodating to anyone. But she had learned enough about people during her time as an investigative reporter to know when there was a potential for danger.

"Sorry, waiting for the plumber," she said swiftly and glanced down at her hands. It was a lie, but there was no way she was going to let them get passed her and further into the house. She was certain there was something off about them. She had the same uneasy feeling she had when she found the fingerprints and when she was in the library.

"Did you hear that, Al?" George asked as he looked over at the skinny man. "She's waiting on the plumber," he chuckled as if that was some kind of inside joke between the two men and then shook his head as he walked out through the door. Al followed close behind him, slamming the screen door shut as he left. Suzie was so relieved to see them go that she quickly closed and locked the door. She was used to working with the door open so that people could come and go as they pleased, but she realized she might have to change that policy.

She was still a little unnerved by the visit from the strange men when she heard a pounding on the door. She looked up from the table she had been cleaning and stared at the door. She waited to see if whoever was knocking would leave.

"Suzie?" Mary called through the door. "Are you in there?"

Suzie smiled and walked over to open the door. Mary looked confused as she stepped inside and Suzie took one of the bags of groceries that Mary was carrying.

"Why was the door locked?" she asked as she followed after Suzie with the other bag of groceries.

"I'm sorry, I just had a strange visit from two men, and I felt uncomfortable leaving it unlocked," Suzie explained as she began pulling the cold and frozen items out of the bags.

"Two men?" Mary asked and began taking the canned food out. "What was strange about them?"

"They wanted to rent a room," Suzie muttered as she stacked the last of the frozen food in the freezer. Mary had bought much more than the items she had gone out for.

"Well, that's not so strange, it is a B & B after all," Mary replied with a short laugh.

"I know, but it was the way they spoke to me," Suzie shivered a little. "Their eyes were just..." she hesitated for a moment as she tried to come up with the right word.

"Mean? Cold?" Mary suggested and finished stacking the cans.

"Cruel," Suzie said with a light snap of her fingers. "That's it, they were cruel."

"Oh, that doesn't sound good at all," Mary said with a frown. "Maybe we should have Jason come by and check things out? Or at least let him know?"

"No, I don't think we need to get Jason involved," Suzie shook her head. "I don't want to go running to him all the time. He has a very busy life," she muttered.

"Hmm," Mary folded up the cloth grocery bags and tucked them in the cabinet beside the refrigerator. "Well, if you see them again you need to say something. And from now on we'll keep that door locked. This might be a small town, but crime still does happen."

"Yes, at least until we open," Suzie agreed. But as she stared wistfully through the tall kitchen windows she found herself wondering if that would be enough. She still felt a sense of discomfort, and she simply couldn't shake it.

"Do you think that the weather will be clear enough tomorrow for us to go on our treasure hunt?" Mary asked. Suzie could tell she was hoping to distract her from the current topic.

"I hope so," Suzie said.

"I'm still not so sure about getting on that boat," Mary winced.

"It'll be fine," Suzie promised her and offered a warm smile. "I know that you're not a fan of being out on the open water, but I think if you give it a chance you might actually enjoy yourself. It won't be anything like the cruise, I promise," Suzie added.

"I find that very hard to believe," Mary said with a raised eyebrow.

"Well, I don't think Paul is going to serve bad seafood and insist on line dancing," Suzie pointed out with a grin.

"I bet you wouldn't mind too much if he did," Mary winked at her.

"Paul is just a friend," Suzie stated firmly but

she had to turn away from Mary to hide the blush rising in her cheeks.

***

That night Suzie could barely sleep. Every time she closed her eyes she saw George and Al blocking the doorway of Dune House. When she finally fell asleep the dream she found herself in was unsettling. She was on the boat, Paul was smiling at her. Mary was waving at her with a big grin. It was a beautiful day. The sky was clear. But Suzie was feeling uneasy. She looked up at the sky to see a swirling tornado headed straight towards them.

Neither of them seemed to notice the certain disaster that was headed straight for them.

Somewhere in the back of her mind she knew it couldn't be real, but it was happening right before her eyes.

"Mary!" she cried out. Her voice woke her from her sleep. She sat straight up in bed.

"Suzie?" Mary said as she burst into her room.

"Are you okay?" she asked when she sat down beside Suzie on the bed.

Suzie drank in the sight of Mary with great relief. "I'm sorry, Mary, I just had a bad dream."

"Oh, Suzie, it's okay," Mary promised her and hugged her gently. She studied Suzie with deep concern in her eyes. "Do you want to tell me about it?"

"I..." Suzie opened her mouth to speak further, but something stopped her. She didn't want to tell Mary what she had seen. "I don't want to get on that boat today."

"Suzie, don't say that," Mary frowned. "Weren't you the one telling me that everything would be fine?"

"What if the weather is bad?" Suzie pointed out with anxiety in her voice.

"The weather is perfect," Mary said firmly. "And like you said Paul would never let us out on the water if he thought it was the slightest bit dangerous. You're just under a bit of stress, Suzie, and that can make your mind create some wild things in your sleep."

"I'm sure you're right," Suzie frowned. She wanted to believe that, too. But her dream had her rattled. "We have some time this morning. I think I do want to go and talk to Jason," she said with a heavy sigh.

"About the two men yesterday?" Mary asked.

"About Alexandria Black," Suzie said with a slight shake of her head. "For some reason I can't get her out of my head. I don't think I'm going to be able to get any rest until I do."

"All right," Mary nodded. "Let's head for the police station first thing, okay? I've already got some coffee going."

"Thanks, Mary," Suzie said and hugged her friend.

***

After they had their coffee and a quick bite to eat, Suzie and Mary headed back into town. The rain had died down to a light drizzle, and the roads were clear of any debris. The waves were fairly calm, and Suzie was sure that Paul would be ready to take the boat out. The day before that was all she was hoping for, but after her dream, she was dreading getting out onto the water.

The police station was quiet as it always seemed to be. Suzie held the door open for Mary as they stepped inside. There was a police officer snoozing behind the large front desk. Other officers were milling about near the coffee pot. Suzie spotted Jason leaning over a desk discussing something with a man in plain clothes, who she assumed to be a detective.

"Maybe we shouldn't bother him," Mary said hesitantly. "He looks like he's busy."

"Busy discussing fantasy football or something like that I'm sure," Suzie said with a wink. She waved to Jason until her movement got his attention. He glanced up at her with surprise at first and then smiled as he walked over.

"What are you up to today, Suzie?" he asked

and nodded politely at Mary.

"I was wondering if you could fill us in on some details about a case," Suzie said eagerly. Jason ran his hand back over his cropped red hair and studied the two intently.

"What kind of case?" he asked.

"Robbery," Mary said quickly.

"Murder," Suzie replied.

Jason's eyes widened. "I thought you were going to ask me about trespassing or something, what are you two involved in?"

"Well, we stumbled across something very interesting," Suzie admitted. She studied her cousin intently. She didn't know him very well, but so far he had demonstrated that she could trust him. Still, she proceeded with caution. "It's a painting that belongs to a local artist," she explained. "We wanted to know more about her, so we began searching for information. Her story is very intriguing, and we were just hoping that you might be able to fill in some of the gaps."

"What local artist?" Jason asked, though his gaze was skeptical as he looked between the two. "Why do I feel like you're not telling me the whole story?"

"Alexandria Black," Mary said quickly before Jason could investigate their intent any further.

"Oh," he nodded and then glanced over his shoulder at the other officers. "That's a bit of a ghost story around here."

"Is it?" Suzie asked as she leaned a little closer to him. "How about the husband? Darren Black?"

Jason shifted uncomfortably and then steered Suzie and Mary over towards a quiet corner.

"Listen, I was a bit younger than Alexandria at school and Darren only moved to Garber when he married Alexandria. I didn't really know them but I knew of them. As you both know, this is a town that doesn't like its dirty laundry aired," he looked directly at Suzie. "If you have questions I'll do my best to answer them, but it's best to keep this as quiet as possible."

"Why?" Suzie asked. "I don't understand why it's such a big issue?"

"We don't see a lot of crime in this town," Jason explained and rested his hand lightly on the gun holstered at his hip. "So, when one of the locals commits suicide not long after her husband committed an armed robbery, it was just one of those things that everyone did their best to avoid talking about."

"Sounds a little behind the times," Mary said with a slight frown.

"Maybe so," Jason nodded. "But the point is, if you want to get along well in this town, you don't want to create a stir."

"I see what you're saying," Suzie nodded. "And honestly I'm not trying to. But I would like to know more about Alexandria's death."

Jason furrowed his eyebrows and studied his cousin with disbelief. "She threw herself off a cliff, what more is there to know?" he asked.

"If she really did throw herself off a cliff,"

Suzie replied with confidence.

"What are you talking about?" Jason asked with a little anger rising in his voice. "Are you trying to say that her death was somehow covered up?"

"No, I'm not saying that at all," Suzie replied swiftly as she realized she might have offended him. "It's just that in my experience sometimes what looks like a suicide, might not be a suicide."

He narrowed his eyes a little further and then nodded slowly. "I guess in some cases that might be true, but I doubt it is in this case."

"Why?" Mary asked. "Is there something about the case that makes you certain it was a suicide?"

"Well, she left a note," Jason said with a frown. "It's pretty evident that when someone leaves a note their intent was to say goodbye."

"I didn't realize she left a note," Suzie said with some disappointment. "Do you still have it?"

"I'm sure we have a copy in her file," Jason

said with a sigh. "I'll go get it."

"Thanks Jason," Suzie replied with a smile

He nodded as he walked away.

"I guess she really did commit suicide," Mary said softly.

"It sure looks that way," Suzie admitted. "But I still wonder what happened to that money. Maybe the note will give us some kind of clue."

"Here, let's go sit at that table over there," Jason said with the files in his hands as he pointed to a small table and chairs at the far side of the station. The three walked over to the table.

Once they were settled Jason flipped open Alexandria's file.

"Here's the note," Jason said. It was a short, handwritten note that seemed to be straight to the point. "Goodbye world, goodbye pain," Jason read in a quiet voice.

"That's it?" Mary asked with surprise.

"Seems to be," Jason replied matter-of-factly.

"Well, I guess it sums everything up," Mary pointed out mildly.

"Does it though? I mean why go to all the trouble of writing a note, if you're not going to give some explanation of why you were jumping to your death?" Suzie shook her head. "It still doesn't sit right with me."

"Suicide sometimes has no explanation," Mary frowned. "People make impulsive choices. Maybe she just decided she was done with life, and scribbled out a note in case no one found her."

"Maybe," Suzie sighed. "Is there anything of interest in Darren's file?"

"He was arrested along with two other men," Jason said as he opened the file on the table in front of him. "It looks like they'd been planning this for some time. He got the most time out of all three because the other two insisted he was the mastermind of the plan. However, he denied that."

"Two against one is not favorable odds," Suzie

said with a slight shake of her head. Then she looked down at the file. The faces of the three men that stared up at her were slightly distorted by the poor quality of the prints, but there was no mistaking what she saw. She held her breath as she didn't want to tell Jason what she recognized in front of her.

"There's a phone call for you, Jason," one of the officers called out to him.

"I'll be back in a second," Jason said as he closed the files and walked over to his desk to take the call.

"Mary!" Suzie gasped, and then covered her mouth when several officers looked in their direction. "Those two men with Darren in the photograph were the two men who came to the house yesterday," she hissed. "Their names were Al and George."

"Are you sure?" Mary asked as she slid her chair closer to Suzie's. "Their names were different in the file."

"I'm sure they were using aliases," Suzie said and narrowed her eyes. "I know it was them. I'd know those eyes anywhere."

"Yes, they were quite menacing," Mary agreed as she recalled the two men in the photograph. "To think you were alone with two criminals!" she frowned.

"But why were they there?" Suzie asked. "That's the important question. Obviously they weren't there just to rent a room."

"Are you thinking that they were looking for the map?" Mary asked with a tremor of fear in her voice. "That they're after the money that Alexandria hid?"

"The map or something else that would lead them to the money," Suzie pointed out. "It's the only thing that makes sense. They must have found out we bought the painting for Dune House and were trying to get to it."

"To be fair, they did grow up nearby. Maybe they were just visiting for old time's sake? How could they know that we had purchased the painting?" Mary asked skeptically. "Unless," her voice trailed off for a moment. "I guess that Luther could have told someone."

"Small town, big ears," Suzie reminded her. "Word travels fast, too. Maybe they heard about Alexandria's possessions going on sale and decided to show up to purchase them in the hope that something would give them a clue. But when they arrived we had already purchased the painting, so they wanted to rent a room in the house in the hope of getting a closer look at it."

"Or even so that they could steal the painting," Mary said quietly. "Oh, how frightening, to think that we could have been sleeping under the same roof as those awful men," she growled and shook her head. "I have no patience for thieves. I'm sorry you faced them alone, Suzie."

"It's okay," Suzie shook her head with a gasp. "I'm sure they were spying on me through the kitchen window, and then again at the library.

They must be following us all around town!" She glanced up quickly to survey everyone who was in the police station. But all of the men and women she saw were either in uniform, or people she recognized.

"That's probably why they came while I was gone!" Mary groaned. "They must have been watching and saw that you were alone."

"Well, if they are here for the map, then they are not going to stop looking for the map, or the money," Suzie said with a frown. "We need to figure out where that map leads and fast," she glanced at her watch and then nodded. "We've got an hour before we're supposed to meet Paul at the docks. There's one more thing I want to look into," she said as she stood up from the table and Jason hung up the phone and started walking towards them.

"Sorry about that. Is there anything else you need?" he offered as he reached the table.

"Tell him, Suzie," Mary prompted her friend.

Jason looked at Suzie expectantly. His serious expression, and the badge shimmering on his chest made Suzie hesitate. She was afraid that if she told him the truth, about the map and the men searching for it, he would demand that she turn over the map and prevent her from finding out where it led.

"Tell me what?" Jason asked, his eyes narrowing as he studied Suzie. "Is there something I should know?" he pressed when she didn't answer right away. "Is it about Dune House?" he asked.

"No," Suzie shook her head quickly. Jason should have been the one to inherit Dune House, but his father had left it to Suzie instead. Although Jason seemed to be fine with that, she sometimes wondered if he really was. "Nothing is wrong with the house. Just a silly suspicion I have," she shrugged mildly. "I'll let you know if it turns into something more."

Mary frowned as she glanced at Suzie. Jason looked over at Mary and stared at her for a long moment before looking back at Suzie.

"You do that," he said firmly. "I don't want either of you getting into trouble, if you need anything, just ask me, okay?" he looked at the two of them but his eyes came to rest on Suzie. He had a powerful gaze, it was one of the first things she had noticed about him, as it reminded her of the few times when as a child she had met his father.

"We will," Suzie nodded, but she had no intention of asking for his help.

As they left the police station Mary spoke in a hushed voice. "Why didn't you tell him about Al and George, Suzie?" she asked. "He might have been able to help us."

"Mary, Jason is a wonderful man, and he is a wonderful police officer," Suzie said as they reached the car. "But he is still just that, a police officer. If you want to get to the bottom of things, sometimes you have to leave the law out of it. If I told him about Al and George he'd want to have someone watching Dune House, and he'd want to know about the map. If I gave him the map, we'd never be able to find out where it led."

"But maybe he'd want to search with us," Mary pointed out with a frown as she climbed into the car.

"Maybe," Suzie said and started the engine. "But, maybe he wouldn't. Maybe he would feel obligated to turn the information over, and then we would be left without our adventure, and without the proof we need to show that Alexandria didn't kill herself."

"We still don't know that to be the case," Mary reminded Suzie as Suzie pulled out of the parking lot of the police station and began driving down the road.

"Exactly," Suzie said glumly. "And how long do you think Al and George would get for asking for a room at Dune House?" Suzie pointed out. "They haven't actually done anything wrong."

"That's true," Mary said softly. "Nothing we can prove anyway."

"The first thing we need to do is find a way to show that Alexandria didn't jump, and the best way to get that information is to see Dr. Rose," Suzie said with confidence.

"Dr. Rose? The medical examiner?" Mary asked with surprise. "I doubt she worked the case, she's so young herself."

"No, probably not, but she'll have access to the records," Suzie said as she drove towards the county morgue.

Chapter Five

Mary shivered slightly as Suzie parked outside the county morgue. Mary had an aversion to morgues. The morgue had recently moved from the basement of the police station to a new building on the outskirts of town.

"Let's go have a chat, hmm?" Suzie said as she opened the car door.

"First you want me to go to prison, now this," Mary said with a shake of her head. "I'm starting to think you're a bad influence, Suzie."

"You're just realizing that now?" Suzie grinned at her friend and they walked towards the morgue. It was very quiet, without even a receptionist behind the desk.

"Hello?" Suzie called out, but not too loudly. It seemed wrong to shout in such a quiet place.

"Listen," Mary said. "I can hear music."

Suzie listened and heard the faint music

coming from behind the double doors that led to the examining room.

"Hello?" Suzie called out again as she walked towards the doors. "Dr. Rose, are you here?" she asked.

Suzie could hear the music more clearly when she pushed open the double doors, but she still didn't see Dr. Rose. The lights were bright in the examination room. There were a few empty gurneys in the center of the room. Suzie was relieved that they were empty.

"Is she in there?" Mary asked from outside the doors. "Is anyone in there?" she added with more fear in her voice.

"It doesn't look like anyone is," Suzie said with a frown. "Hello? Dr. Rose?" she called out loudly.

Suddenly a door at the other end of the examination room swung open, and what stepped through was more than a little startling. A figure with a plastic covering over its face and head-to-

toe coveralls. The figure froze in the doorway as the music flooded the room.

"Suzie?" a female voice asked as she lifted the plastic covering up above her head. "Is that you?"

"Yes," Suzie said with relief in her voice when she recognized Dr. Rose. "I'm sorry I know I probably shouldn't be back here, but we didn't see anyone and..."

"I told the receptionist to take the day off," Dr. Rose said with a wave of her hand. "I only had one exam to do, and she had some damage from that storm yesterday. What can I help you with?" she asked as she tugged her gloves off and tossed them in a bio-hazard trash can. Suzie gulped as she realized that Dr. Rose was likely conducting an autopsy in the next room. "Sorry about the music," she added. "It helps me stay focused."

"Oh, it's fine," Suzie nodded with a faint smile. "I'm sorry to bother you. I was just wondering if I could ask you a few questions."

"About what?" Dr. Rose asked as she gestured

to the double doors. "Why don't we talk up front?" she suggested.

"Yes," Suzie nodded and pushed the door open for Dr. Rose. Her dark blonde hair was pulled back into a tight bun at the back of her head and covered by a hair net. From previous experience Suzie knew that Dr. Rose took her job very seriously. She wondered if she'd be willing to part with any information about Alexandria's death.

Mary was still standing nervously outside the doors. She had her hands clasped together in front of her, and Suzie could see that she was uncomfortable.

"Hi Mary," Dr. Rose said with a smile. "Good to see you."

"You too," Mary replied and tried to ignore the faint splattering of blood on Dr. Rose's coveralls.

"So, what questions do you have?" Dr. Rose asked as she paused beside the front desk.

"Well, we recently purchased a painting by a local artist, Alexandria Black," Suzie explained. "We'd just like to know a little bit more about how she passed."

"Why?" Dr. Rose asked with a slightly furrowed brow. "Was she a friend?"

"Not exactly," Suzie frowned. "But her painting is very intriguing, and we thought it would be a story that we could share with our guests."

"Well, I don't know how good a story it would be," Dr. Rose shook her head. "Alexandria Black killed herself, I believe," she frowned as if she was trying to remember.

"That was the original finding," Suzie said cautiously. "But is there any possibility that could be a mistake?" she asked.

Dr. Rose's eyes flashed with interest. She leaned over the computer, careful not to touch anything with her coveralls.

"Let me take a look here," she murmured.

"Hmm, there doesn't seem to be a digital record. Must have been before the conversion."

"Oh well," Mary said with a frown. "I guess we should just go then," she gave Suzie's arm a little tug.

"No, we can just do this the old fashioned way," Dr. Rose said. "Alexandria Black, yes, I read about this case," Dr. Rose said as she glanced over at her filing cabinet. "I was still a student when this happened, but it was one of the cases I was given to study since it was so simple," she reached into the filing cabinet and pulled out one of the files. "Alexandria Black, suicide," she scanned the document. "Nothing unusual," she said with a slight shrug.

"And there was never a question that it was a suicide?" Suzie pressed with disbelief. "Even though she hadn't shown signs of depression?"

"Most people don't show signs of depression," Dr. Rose said with a frown. "I've rarely seen a suicide case where the family wasn't shocked. No one expects anyone to take their own life," she added.

"But still, there weren't any unusual cuts or bruising?" Suzie asked insistently.

"Well, of course there were many bruises and cuts, she landed on the rocks below," Dr. Rose explained. "But nothing that was suspicious." Dr. Rose looked up at her curiously. "Do you have reason to think it was?"

"I just have a little hunch," Suzie replied in an innocent tone. "It just seems so odd to me."

"As I said before, no one really expects it," Dr. Rose replied with a mild shrug.

"But there were no strange marks, nothing at all?" Suzie continued, she had hoped that there would be something in the file that revealed the truth, or what she believed to be the truth.

Mary was trying to get a look at the file itself when Dr. Rose closed the file with a swift snap.

"To be honest there was one thing that I was a little unsettled by when I reviewed the case in class," she said softly. "I dismissed it at the time because my teacher didn't seem to think it was of any interest."

"What was it?" Mary asked, and Suzie looked at Dr. Rose eagerly.

"Not to be too graphic," Dr. Rose warned, "but in most suicides that are jumpers, the person lands with the body towards the ground," she explained. "Alexandria was found face up in the water. It was assumed that she had flipped over as she fell, which is a little unusual from that height, she didn't have much time between leaving the cliff, and hitting the rocks and water to do a full somersault."

"So, then it's possible that someone pushed her?" Suzie asked her eyes wide.

"Not really," Dr. Rose explained. "When someone is pushed, there's usually evidence of it. Either there will be scuffing in the dirt or sand above the cliff, or the person who is pushed will have some torn clothing. Sometimes they are found in a defensive position, like with their hands over their face to shield themselves. Jumpers don't often do that. They know they are falling."

"Alexandria displayed none of that?" Mary asked with a frown.

"No, she didn't have any defensive wounds, the only tearing in her clothing was consistent with her falling, and there were no scuff marks on the cliff. She seemed to have just jumped right off the edge, with no hesitation," she pursed her lips briefly before putting the file back into the filing cabinet. "A very sad case."

"Thank you for your help," Suzie said quietly. "Did you know Alexandria?"

"No, I didn't," Dr. Rose shook her head. "I went to school in the next town over, they just used her case file in my class. I was hired here right out of school, and have been here ever since. I have heard a few stories about Alexandria and seen some of her artwork around town. She was very talented."

"I think so, too," Suzie agreed. "I just wish I could understand what really happened to her."

"You still don't think it was a suicide?" Dr. Rose asked skeptically.

"No," Suzie answered honestly. "I don't."

"Hmm, well if you discover anything, let me know," Dr. Rose nodded. "I'll help you anyway I can."

"Thanks," Suzie said as she and Mary walked towards the door.

"If you see Jason before I do tell him I said hello," Dr. Rose added just as Suzie was opening the door.

"Absolutely," Suzie agreed and stepped the rest of the way out the door.

"Looks like you might not be the only Allen headed for romance," Mary teased as they reached the car.

"That's it!" Suzie declared with humor in her

sharp voice. "No more romances for you. I forbid it!"

"I can read what I please," Mary said with a playful huff. As they drove away from the morgue, Mary spoke softly. "Do you really think it was murder?"

"I do," Suzie said with a sigh. "I can't explain exactly why, but I do."

"Well, in that case we need to be very careful. If Al and George were involved in one murder, they likely wouldn't be opposed to being involved in another."

Mary's words hung heavy in the car. When they pulled up to the docks, Suzie sighed as she put the car in park.

"Puts a little damper on our adventure, doesn't it?" she asked.

"Just a little," Mary agreed. "Why don't you wait here for Paul while I go grab the map?" she suggested. Suzie knew it was a ruse to give her some alone time with Paul, but she didn't complain. She wanted to sort through her thoughts a bit before they embarked on their journey.

"Sounds good," she agreed and handed the keys over.

.

Chapter Six

Suzie stepped out onto the dock. There wasn't a trace of the storm from the day before. The water was calm. She stood on the dock and looked out at the water. The beautiful sky that spread out before her was not a reflection of what she was feeling inside. The only thing she was looking forward to about the trip was seeing Paul again. Her heart fluttered a little with the thought of it. She didn't have long to wait as his car pulled up a few minutes later.

"Hi Suzie," he smiled at her as he walked up the docks. But his smile faded when he saw her expression. "Are you doing okay? The weather is clear if that's what you're worried about," he added.

For just a minute she considered telling him what she had experienced, and her theory about Al and George. But as she stared into his gray gaze, she found herself worried about what he would think of her suspicions. Would he think she was creating wild ideas?

"I'm okay," she finally responded. "I just hope that we're able to find something today."

"We might just find it, with this," Mary said as she hurried up to them with the map in her hand.

"Are you ready for this?" Mary asked as she looked over at Suzie.

Paul was still studying Suzie curiously. Suzie got the feeling that he did not believe what she had said.

"I think so," Suzie sighed as she straightened the collar of her blouse. "Are you?" she asked with some concern.

"If it means finding the truth about Alexandria, then I'm more than ready," Mary said with confidence.

"What do you mean the truth about Alexandria?" Paul asked quizzically as he led them on to his boat.

"Never mind," Suzie waved her hand. "Let's just see where the day leads."

Paul nodded and started the engine of the boat. The water lapped at the boat, rocking it softly. Paul was carefully steering it through the water, but the weather was clear, and the sky did not have a cloud in sight. The memory of her dream flooded Suzie's mind. As she waited for the moment of fear to pass, Suzie clutched tightly to the metal railing that lined the boat. She glanced over at Mary, who seemed to have forgotten about her aversion to boats. She had her face upturned to the wind. Her lips were spread wide with a smile. Suzie admired that carefree expression. It was not what she expected from Mary considering her previous fear of boats. Now she seemed very relaxed and comfortable. It seemed to Suzie that Mary had become more trusting of Paul than even she was.

"Are you ladies doing okay?" Paul called back over his shoulder.

"Wonderful," Mary replied, her face still

turned into the wind.

Suzie couldn't bring herself to speak, she was afraid anything she said might sound foolish.

"Suzie?" Paul asked and looked over at her with growing concern. "Are you all right?"

"Sure, I'm fine," she replied her voice wavering slightly.

"You don't seem fine, you don't seem like yourself at all," Paul said with a frown. "Come over here and join me," he suggested as he looked out across the water again. The boat was skimming the coast as he headed for the inlet he thought the map indicated. Suzie took a deep breath and began to walk along the railing. When she passed by Mary, Mary gave her a light wink.

"It's going to be fine," she whispered to Suzie, but Suzie was already lost in the sight of the water spreading out before her. It was both frightening and soothing which left her feeling quite confused.

"Here you go," Paul said as he reached out

and gently took her hand. Suzie glanced up at him when their hands touched and he smiled warmly at her. "I think you just need to see the water from my point of view," he suggested.

"What do you mean?" Suzie asked as she stepped closer to him. He guided her right in front of him. Then he lifted her hands to the steering wheel of the boat. She felt the subtle vibration beneath her hands and looked out across the water. Paul's hands rested on her wrists a moment longer, and then fell to the wheel on either side of her grasp.

"Look," he murmured as he tilted his head towards the horizon. "Isn't it beautiful?"

Suzie found herself smiling as she looked out across the water. The view seemed to be endless, as the water eventually blended into the sky. It really was quite beautiful. There wasn't a wild tornado in sight. Suzie felt more in control standing at the helm, and she began to slowly relax. Despite the fact that she was feeling calmer, her heart was still racing. She knew that was only because Paul was standing so close.

"Is it far?" she asked over the sound of the engine.

"Not too much further," Paul replied.

"Are you sure it's the right place?" Mary asked. She was still leaning against the railing with her face turned into the wind that the movement of the boat created.

"I would bet my boat on it," Paul said with a glimmer of humor in his voice. "I know these parts pretty well, and that's one area that not too many people go to. If I was going to hide treasure, I'd hide it there."

"Do you think it's treasure?" Suzie asked and narrowed her eyes. "I mean, it could be anything. We have no idea what we might find."

"That's true," Paul agreed as he steered the boat a little closer to the coastline. "But that's what makes things so interesting. Don't you think? The not knowing?" his voice brushed just beside Suzie's ear, causing her to be lulled by the rhythm of it.

Suzie glanced up at him, and locked her eyes briefly with Paul's. She studied him intently before looking away.

"I suppose it is," she replied with a faint smile.

"Hold on, we might have a new mission," Paul said with a grim frown as he spotted something in the water.

"What are you doing?" Suzie asked as Paul steered the boat away from the coast.

"There are some stranded boaters," he explained as he peered out over the water. "We have to pick them up."

"Oh wow, a real life water rescue," Mary said with a grin. Suzie couldn't smile. She knew that Paul was doing the right thing, but it felt very wrong.

"I'm sure it won't be much of a rescue," Paul explained as he pointed to a small row boat in the middle of the water. "It's more likely to be a couple of tourists that weren't prepared for going out on the water. Sometimes they get too far from shore and can't find their way back."

"Can you see who is in the boat?" Suzie asked nervously as she instinctively tucked the map under her shirt.

"Looks like two guys," Paul said mildly. "Sorry for the interruption, but once we get them to shore we can go right back to our treasure hunt."

"Oh, it's no problem," Suzie assured him as Mary walked up to join them. Suzie was trying to get a look at who was on the boat.

"I hope they haven't been stranded for too long," Mary said with a frown.

"Ahoy there!" Paul shouted as he drew close to the small boat. "Need a lift back to shore?" he offered.

The two men were wearing sweatshirts with hoods pulled forward enough to disguise their faces. But Suzie noticed that one was broad and big like a bear, while the other was skinny like a pole.

Suzie's heart flipped. She opened her mouth to say something, but Paul had already pulled them on board.

"No, no," she muttered as she backed away from the two men.

"Suzie, what's wrong?" Mary asked with concern when she noticed Suzie backing away.

"Thanks for the lift," the tall, thin man, Al, said as he pulled back his hood to reveal the plain black baseball cap that he was wearing.

"We'll take it from here," George said gruffly as he glared at Paul.

"What is that supposed to mean?" Paul asked his bushy eyebrows furrowing as he studied the two men.

"Paul, be careful," Suzie hissed as her heart raced.

"Are these the two men?" Mary asked Suzie in a whisper.

"It means, that this boat and everything on it,

now belongs to us," George said sternly.

"Pirates?" Paul demanded as he moved between the two men and Suzie and Mary. "You boys are really out here playing pirates?"

"I'm sorry, I don't see any boys around here," Al said and gritted his teeth. "But George does have a little friend," he tilted his head towards George.

George held up a gun, and pointed it at each of them in turn. "No one has to get hurt," he said roughly. "But this isn't a game." Suzie instinctively looked at her cell phone that was on a bench next to Mary's and Al must have noticed because he swiftly picked the phones up and threw them overboard.

Suzie felt Mary's fingernails digging into her arm as she clung to her. She knew that Mary was terrified. Suzie was pretty frightened herself. But Paul stood his ground, his hands in fists at his sides.

"This is ridiculous, there's nothing on this

boat that you could possibly want," he argued as he looked at the men. "I don't know what you two were planning but I think you must have your wires crossed, and are after the wrong boat."

"Oh, we're on the right boat all right. Aren't we, Suzie?" Al asked as he looked over at her. "When we found out you bought that painting, we thought it would be simple. We'd rent a room and take the painting. But you ruined that, didn't you?" he asked.

Suzie was silent as she looked at the two men.

"So, now we're going to take what's ours," George said and reached out for the steering wheel. "Where's the map?" he demanded.

"Suzie, do you know these men?" Paul asked, obviously trying to catch up.

"We don't have the map," Suzie said sternly. "We're just out for a boating trip for the day. I don't know what map you could possibly be talking about."

Al stared at her for a long moment. Then he

took a step forward, still glaring at her with those cruel eyes.

"Oh, you know about the map, and I know this is no pleasure cruise, you're out here to find the money. But it's mine, not yours," he said sharply.

"There is no map," Suzie said through gritted teeth.

"Just keep going where you were heading, Captain," George said sternly. "No need for chit chat."

Paul met Suzie's eyes briefly and then turned back to look out over the water. He started the boat once more and began steering it in the same direction.

Mary and Suzie stood close together at the back of the boat. Suzie's stomach was churning with guilt. She wondered if she had told Paul about the two men, if he would have hesitated before picking up the stranded boaters. Maybe if she had just been honest she could have prevented the situation. Now, everyone was in danger and she couldn't help but feel it was all because of her. It wasn't long before Paul cut the engine on the boat. They were beside a small dock that jutted out from a private beach.

"This is it," he said quietly.

"Out, everybody," Al snapped and pointed to the dock. "One at a time, and no funny business," he warned. "We are armed."

Mary shuddered as she grasped Suzie's hand and squeezed it. Suzie tried to give her a look of reassurance but she was sure there was terror in her eyes. Carefully Suzie climbed up onto the dock. She turned back to help Mary onto the dock behind her. Paul climbed up after them followed swiftly by Al and George.

"Keep moving," Al said with a growl. "If you don't take us where we want to go you're going to pay the price," he promised them all.

"Look there's no need for this," Paul said gruffly as he turned to face the two men. "Why don't you just let the ladies go, and we'll handle this like men."

"Oh, you want to handle this?" George asked as he waved a gun in Paul's direction. The sight of the weapon was enough to silence Paul, who swallowed thickly and turned to begin walking once more. George hung back to walk behind them while Al walked beside Paul.

Suzie walked across the sand, attempting to keep her legs from buckling. Just knowing that George was walking behind her with a gun in his hand was enough to make her weak with fear. She knew she had to be strong, not just for herself but for Mary and Paul, but her heart was pounding so hard she was sure it would burst.

"Here," Paul said roughly as he suddenly stopped on the sand. "It's close to here."

"Where is it exactly?" Al demanded as he glared at Paul.

"I'm not going to tell you that," Paul said bravely as he turned to face them.

"Are you crazy?" Al demanded and signaled to

George to step closer to him. "If you don't, George is going to make you wish you never woke up this morning," Al warned.

"I'm not going to tell you until you guarantee me that Suzie and Mary will be safe," he finished with certainty. "I'm not going to take you the rest of the way unless I know that they are not going to be harmed."

"Do you really think we're going to let them go?" Al asked as he stepped closer to Paul. "You're nuts. I know that the only reason you're being so compliant is because they are here."

"Then we're at an impasse, because I'm not taking another step until they're safe," he said sternly and folded his arms across his chest. Suzie stared at him with amazement, that he could be so brave in their situation, but her stomach was in knots as she anticipated what might happen.

"Tell you what," Al said thoughtfully. "I'll let one of them go, just to be nice," he smirked as he looked at Paul.

Paul glanced over at Suzie and Mary. Suzie could see the fear in his eyes.

"Just one," Al reminded him. "For your complete cooperation. Understand?" he asked.

"Yes," Paul breathed out.

Mary tightened her grasp on Suzie's hand. Suzie tried not to show any fear as Al began walking towards them.

"All right, the blonde can go," Al said with a shrug. Mary let go of Suzie's hand. Suzie stared at Al with pure animosity.

"I'm not going anywhere," she said sternly. "Mary should go."

"You don't get to decide," Al snapped and drew back his hand as if he might strike her. "This is not up for a vote. You're going. You, I don't trust," he narrowed his eyes at her.

"Mary has a health condition," Suzie said quickly, her heart racing. She couldn't leave Mary behind. She had two children, she had many people that depended on her. Suzie on the other hand, didn't think too many people would miss her. "If she's without her medicine much longer, she'll pass out, and you'll have to carry her..."

"All right, all right," Al snapped.

"Suzie, no," Mary hissed and grabbed her hand again. She clung to it tightly. "I can't leave you here like this."

"You have to," Suzie said sternly and pulled her hand away. "You know what to do, Mary," she locked eyes with her friend and held her gaze intently. "You know what to do," she repeated.

Mary was trembling as she walked off across the sand. Suzie wasn't even sure if Mary knew how to get back to the populated area of the beach. She could only hope that she would.

Chapter Seven

Suzie's eyes were following Mary until she walked out of sight.

"There now, let's get moving," Al said and gave Suzie a little push to her back.

"Watch it," Paul warned.

"Shut your mouth," George ordered and kicked some sand in Paul's direction.

Paul met Suzie's eyes for a moment, and then began walking in the direction of the location he thought the map identified. Suzie tried to concentrate on what lay ahead of her, but her mind kept returning to Mary. She was worried she would get lost.

"It's right down here," Paul said as he began scaling down along the rocky side of a cliff.

"Where are you going?" Al demanded. "Are you trying to make us fall?"

"Look, this is the only way to get to the inlet,"

Paul said sternly.

"Fine," Al said impatiently.

"Careful, Suzie," Paul said as he reached up to help guide her down the face of the rocks.

Suzie did her best to keep her footing but Paul's hand against her back kept her from slipping when she missed one of the rocks that she was climbing down. When they reached the sandy ground below, she found herself gazing into Paul's gray eyes. They were normally cool and impassive, but in that moment they were full of heat. She wasn't sure if it was because of the situation they were in, or because they were so close. She didn't have the chance to find out.

"So, where is it?" Al demanded as he stomped through the sand. "All I see is more sand!"

"It's here," Paul said patiently. "Just around that bend," he pointed to another outcropping of rocks.

"You better not be playing any tricks on me," Al warned. "I'm in no mood for it. I've waited long enough for what is rightfully mine."

Paul looked uneasy as he took Suzie's hand in his and began to lead her along the sand and around the rocks. When they reached the other side there was a long thin inlet of water that was impossible to see from the rocks above. It wound in a lazy pattern from the water's edge.

"This is it?" George asked skeptically. "Are you sure?"

"No, I'm not sure," Paul replied honestly. "I just thought this might be the place, and we were coming to check it out. I have no idea if I was right about it or not."

"Well, what next?" Al asked with a frown. "Where's the map?"

Paul was silent as Al glared at him. Then Al turned his demanding gaze on Suzie.

"Where's the map?" he asked again, with fury rising in his voice.

"I said I didn't have a map..." she began to say, but he snapped his hand directly in front of her face, making her jump with fear.

"Give me the map, or I will take it from you," he warned her.

"Suzie," Paul growled and tightened his grasp on her hand. "Just give it to him," he insisted.

Suzie frowned as she knew that the moment she gave the map to Al, she was going to be useless to him. She presumed that at least they would want to keep Paul alive because they would want to use his boat to transport the money.

There was pleading in Paul's eyes, as if he was silently asking her to trust him. She had never been one to trust easily, considering the things she had witnessed in her life. But there was something about Paul that made her instinctively certain that he had her best interests at heart. Reluctantly, Suzie pulled the map out from under her shirt. In a trembling hand she passed it over to Al.

"Here it is, finally," Al said with joy in his voice. "You're much wiser than Alexandria," he said with a slight shake of his head. "If she would have just given us this map years ago, none of us would be in this mess."

"You didn't have to kill her," Suzie suddenly stated. "She was barely more than a child."

"It was an accident," George said quietly.

"Shut up, George!" Al shouted. "You don't want to give them more ammunition. Just keep your mouth shut."

"I'm sure it was no accident when you shoved her off that cliff," Suzie challenged, her attention now focusing on George.

"Suzie," Paul breathed her name as a warning and she felt his grip tighten on her hand. But it was too late for Suzie to turn back. If she was going to die, she was going to at least find out the truth.

"First you threw Darren under a bus. You claimed it was his plan, but it never was, was it?" she demanded. "You let him take the fall, because you wanted to get to that money before he could."

Al was looking over the map intently. "This is gibberish," he complained. "It doesn't make any sense."

George was still staring straight into Suzie's eyes. It was clear that he was eager to confess to his transgressions.

"Darren was just a kid, he didn't need all that money," he muttered. "Besides Al and I did all the work. All he did was drive the getaway car. When everything was going down he told us his wife knew some places that she could stash the cash. So we let him give it to her. But he was only living in Garber for a short time and he never knew exactly where the money was. Said his wife had left a map hidden for him so if something happened to her before he was released he would be able to find the money. But he wouldn't tell us where the map was, he just said that he knew the money was buried near the cliffs in Garber but nothing more."

"Because he knew," Suzie said with confidence. "He knew that you two would try to con him out of his share, so the location was known by the only person he ever trusted, his young wife, who you hunted down and murdered..."

"No!" George fumed as Al looked up from the map. "It was an accident!" he insisted. "I went to grab her and..."

"George!" Al spat his name out and glared at him. "Shut up already! You don't have to answer to her! She's nobody!"

"But you do have to answer to Alexandria, don't you?" Suzie pressed as Paul observed, his lips half-open with shock at the way she was interrogating George. "And Darren, who was killed in prison because you two pinned the crime on him and he served more time. Now, you think you deserve the money you stole and murdered for?"

"All I did was reach for her," George admitted, Suzie was surprised to see tears in his eyes. "She was running from me, she was scared. I reached for her, I wasn't going to hurt her, but she lunged out of my way and went right over the side of the cliff," his eyes widened in horror as if he was reliving the moment. "I didn't push her," he breathed out, his voice trembling. "I didn't even touch her."

"And that absolves you?" Suzie asked, her voice softer but filled with hatred. "Did you see the shock in her eyes when she was falling, George? Was that worth the money that never even belonged to you?"

"I," George swallowed thickly and closed his eyes. That was the moment that Suzie had been waiting for. The moment he closed his eyes, Suzie lunged forward and released Paul's hand. She shoved her full body weight against George, which wasn't much considering he was built like a mountain, and at the same time grabbed the barrel of the gun he was holding. The surprise he experienced at the sudden blow was exactly what Suzie had been hoping for. He released his grasp on the gun for just a split-second, but it was long enough for Suzie to wrench it from his hand.

"Hey!" Al shouted when he saw what was happening. He tucked the map into his pocket as he lunged for Suzie. Paul was already in the middle of the fray as he tried to deflect Al from grasping Suzie's arm. The four engaged in a tangle of fists, shouts, and grunts as they struggled over the weapon. Suzie's heart was pounding, and each beat sounded like a gunshot in her ears. She knew that the trigger could be pulled at any moment. She knew that she might have made her final mistake. When she broke free of George she still had the gun in her hand. She raised it as she backed away from the men. She pointed it in the direction of George and Al. Al had his arm slung around Paul's neck and was squeezing.

"Let him go!" she demanded in the strongest voice she could muster.

"Drop the gun," Al challenged, his eyes as hard as granite. "Or I slice his throat."

Only then did Suzie see the small blade in Al's

hand. He had it pressed against the side of Paul's throat. Her heart immediately sunk. She knew the moment she dropped the gun it would likely be retrieved and used against her. It was not a risk she could take. But she also couldn't let Paul get hurt because of her reckless move. She stared into Paul's eyes, and though she knew he had to be terrified, he offered her a small smile of reassurance.

"It's okay, Suzie, shoot the scumbag," he said in a clear even tone.

Suzie raised the gun and pointed it right at Al's head. Her hand was shaking, but her finger was on the trigger.

"Drop the knife and let him go," she said in a stern voice.

"Like you're going to let him die," Al chuckled. "Do you think he really wants to die for you?" he asked.

"Are you going to let him die for you?" Suzie suddenly asked and then pointed the gun directly at George.

"Drop it!" Al shouted in a panic. Suzie had noticed that Al was protective of George and tolerant of him even when he made mistakes. She presumed that their bond had to be strong for Al to put up with him and want to share the money with him.

"Let him go," Suzie said, struggling to keep the fear out of her voice. "Let Paul go, and I'll drop the gun."

"Or you'll shoot us both," Al shouted back, obviously beginning to unravel.

"I'm not a murderer," Suzie said calmly. "I'm not going to kill anyone."

"Sure," Al spat back. "George, get the gun from her. She's not going to kill anyone, right?" he said and glanced over at George.

Paul seized the moment to grab the hand that was holding the blade at his throat. He pulled at it hard, and Al's skinny frame was no match for Paul's powerful muscles. He tugged hard and flung Al over his shoulder twisting his body to encourage the tumble. Al landed hard on the ground and the blade was knocked right out of his hand.

Suzie scrambled for the blade, and in the process, George grabbed hold of her from behind. He wrenched the gun from her hand, twisting her wrist backward so far that a cry of pain escaped from her lips. He fired off a warning shot straight up into the air.

"Stop all of this now!" he demanded. He pointed the gun directly at Suzie. "Pick up the blade, Al," he said calmly as he glared at Paul daring him to make a move.

Suzie felt her heart sink as she realized that their only chance to escape had just been wasted. George released the safety as he continued to point the gun at Suzie.

"Shoot her," Al snapped as he brushed sand off his clothes. "We have the map now, we don't need her. We've still got him to operate the boat."

"No!" Paul shouted abruptly and lunged towards Suzie. Suzie was frozen where she stood as the sound of the safety being released had made the fact that she was staring down the barrel of a loaded gun quite real.

"Don't," George warned as he swung the gun towards Paul and then pointed it right back at Suzie again. "I'm not shooting anybody," he said firmly. "Everyone just calm down, you too, Al."

"Don't tell me to calm down..." Al began to shout.

"This is how it happened last time," George argued. "You promised me no one would have to die this time. Now, as long as they do as they're asked, they shouldn't have to die."

Al rolled his eyes and waved his hand dismissively. "Whatever you say, George. Let's just get the cash and get moving before that gunshot gets the attention of the local cops."

"All right, all right," George nodded and gestured with the gun towards Paul. "Move it, take us to the cash before I let Al call the shots again."

Paul lowered his eyes and reached for Suzie's hand, but George shoved his hand away before Paul could grasp it. "No more touchy feely," he insisted. "Just keep walking."

Paul glanced up at Suzie briefly, and Suzie saw the pain in his eyes. She knew then that he was sure they were not going to get away. He turned and began walking across the sand.

"There's a small cavern inside the rocks," Paul explained quietly as they reached another outcropping of rocks. "It's just about there," he said as he pointed to a small opening in the rocks.

"Just about?" Al growled. "Show me exactly where," he demanded. "You, keep that gun on her, if he tries anything, pull the trigger!" he ordered George.

George pointed the gun at Suzie again and Suzie felt a shiver climb along her spine. His eyes were just as cruel as they had been when she had first met him.

137

Paul spared one more glance in her direction before following Al's command and walking carefully up to the opening in the rocks. He tugged at the cluster of rocks pulling the larger ones free and knocking the smaller ones loose to tumble down along the cliff face. Soon a cavern about the size of a small oven was revealed.

"Is it in there?" Al asked with excitement as he leaned towards the opening.

"I can't tell, it's too dark," Paul said as he peered inside as well.

Al pulled a flashlight from his pocket and shone it inside the cavern. "I think there's something at the back. It looks like a piece of wood sticking straight up. I think it has a star drawn on it," he said in a whisper. He stood back up and pulled out the treasure map from his pocket. He looked at the map. "The star looks exactly like this one," he said as he pointed to a big star drawn at the top of the treasure map. "I bet you the money is buried under it. I am going to have to crawl in," he paused a moment and then shook his head.

"No, you," he pointed to Suzie. "Get inside there and start digging."

Suzie hesitated. She didn't like enclosed spaces. She also didn't like a gun being pointed at her.

"Now!" Al barked.

Suzie moved carefully towards the opening. She could feel Paul's watchful eyes on her.

"Watch it, there are some sharp edges," Paul warned her.

"Quiet," Al snapped. George turned the gun on Paul to keep him quiet.

"I can't get to the back," Suzie said, her voice muffled as she was half-way inside the opening. The truth was she could easily get all the way in. But she knew the moment the money was in Al's hands they had nothing to keep them alive.

"Go in more," Al said and gave her backside a shove.

"Don't!" Paul started to say but George stuck the gun right in his face to quiet him.

"Ouch," Suzie moaned loudly. "I think I'm stuck!"

"Are you serious?" Al demanded and stomped his feet in the sand. "This is insane! Get inside, get to the back!" he shouted again.

"I can't," Suzie insisted and wiggled her legs a little. "I'm completely stuck! You're going to have to pull me out."

Al looked up at the sky and let out a string of curses. "Unbelievable," he finally sighed. "We'll just have to get some of these other rocks out of the way."

He began tugging at the rocks surrounding Suzie. Suzie knew that if he figured out she wasn't actually stuck, he was going to be enraged. She did her best to pretend she was trying to get free.

"Get over here and help!" Al demanded. George lowered the gun and walked over to Al to help him pull out the rocks. "Not you," Al growled.

140

"Him!"

Paul walked up on the other side of Al.

"Are you okay, Suzie?" he asked with concern.

Al interrupted before Suzie could answer. "Listen to me, pal, if we don't get her out of here, I'll take her out piece by piece! So, stop talking and start pulling!"

Paul tugged at the rocks around Suzie's body. She felt his fingers run along her hips, where she was pretending to be wedged. She knew he knew that she wasn't really stuck.

"Maybe we should just think about this for a moment," Paul suggested. "If we get some wet sand, maybe we can pack it around her and..."

"Drop the weapon!" a voice boomed above them. Suzie tensed as she heard the voice. She had no idea who it was, because the rocks muffled the sound of it. She wondered if it could be another criminal there to find the cash.

"Down on your knees!" the voice shouted.

Suzie heard a gunshot, and immediately cried out. "Paul? Paul, are you okay?" she asked as she struggled to back out of the hole she had crawled into.

"Suzie, don't move!" she heard Paul say, but she couldn't be sure if he was hurt or not, she couldn't hear or see anything and she was beginning to panic.

"Paul?" she called out again, though she kept still. "Paul?" she gasped.

"It's okay, Suzie, it's okay," Paul said. "Just be as still as you can, okay? Can you do that for me?"

"Yes, yes," she said quickly, relieved to hear him speak again.

"When they pulled out the other rocks they shifted the weight of the rocks above you," Paul explained as calmly as he could. "So, if you move too much, they might come down on top of you."

"Paul? Who's there? Who shot the gun?" she asked quickly as the danger of her situation began to fully sink in.

"It's me, Jason," she heard the other voice say. "It's okay, Suzie, I've got Al and George in handcuffs. Just be still while we figure out how to get you out of there."

"Okay," Suzie said and tried to hold back the tears that were forming. She felt something sliding in along her back.

"We're putting a wedge in, so that we can make sure the rocks will stay in place," Paul explained. She felt his hand come to rest on her hip. She knew he was just trying to reassure her, and the warmth, the connection, was exactly what she needed to relax and focus on what needed to be done. "Okay, when I say go, I want you to try to move, just a little bit at a time, okay?"

"Okay," Suzie replied and cringed.

"Go!" Paul said. Suzie started to back out, but she was startled when four strong hands seized her on either side of her hips. She was tugged out within the span of a second, and the rocks that had been above her came collapsing down to fill the empty space she had been occupying. Suzie gasped with fear as she stumbled backward and right into Paul's arms. He held her close as he felt her shaking.

"It's okay, you're safe," he murmured and smoothed a hand down through her hair. Suzie's mind was spinning with the remainder of panic, as well as the strange sensation of being engulfed by Paul's strong arms.

"Oh, Suzie, are you okay?" Mary asked as she ran up to her and hugged her tightly. She didn't care that she was sandwiching Suzie between herself and Paul. "I'm sorry, I moved as fast as I could, and I was so scared that I would be too late."

"You were right on time, Mary," Suzie promised her. "You did good," she added as Mary released her, and Paul did as well.

"Are you hurt?" he asked as he looked into her eyes.

"No, I think I'm okay," Suzie replied and

glanced over at the two men cuffed and sitting in the sand.

"They're facing kidnapping and attempted murder," Jason said quickly. "They're not going to be able to bother you anymore."

"You can add murder to that list," Suzie said boldly as she glared at the two men. "They're responsible for Alexandria Black's death, and I'll be happy to testify about what they told me."

Jason raised his eyebrows, adjusted his hat, and turned to glare at the two men.

"There will be time for all of that later, Suzie," Paul assured her. "Now, let's just get you home, hmm?"

Suzie nodded as she suddenly felt exhausted. With everything that had unfolded her adrenaline had been pumping, and now she was ready to crash.

"Are you three okay to travel back on the boat?" Jason asked. "If not I can get a car for you."

"It's fine with me," Suzie murmured. "Are you

up for it, Mary?" she asked.

"After today I think I'd rather be on a boat than on the beach," Mary laughed nervously.

"I'll get them home safe," Paul assured Jason. As they began to walk back towards the boat, Suzie paused and glanced over her shoulder.

"Jason, what about the money?" she asked.

"Well, if it's in there, we'll find it," Jason said with confidence. "I can get somebody out here to dig it up."

"See boys?" Suzie said as she glanced at the two men sitting in the sand. "That money never did, and never will belong to you."

Al snarled but a glare of warning from Jason silenced him. George was just staring at the sand desolately.

When they reached the boat, Paul helped Mary and then Suzie on board. As soon as the boat launched, Mary turned towards Suzie.

"Don't you ever do that to me again," she said

with fury in her eyes.

"What?" Suzie asked with surprise and no small amount of fear. Mary was rarely angry, but when she was, it was a good idea to take cover.

"You made me leave in your place. I would never have forgiven myself if something had happened to you," Mary gulped out and hugged Suzie tightly. Suzie melted into the hug and hugged her friend in return.

"The only thing that kept me sane was knowing that you were safe," Suzie whispered. "I never had any doubt that you would find help."

"That's not a good enough excuse," Mary insisted and released Suzie. She took a step back and placed both of her hands on her hips. "You promise me that you will never ever do that to me again."

Suzie couldn't help but laugh a little as she shook her head. "All right fine, Mary. If armed men ever abduct us again, you can stay behind next time."

"Don't laugh, I'm serious," Mary scoffed and crossed her arms.

"Ladies, why don't we plan on there being no more abductions, wouldn't that be better?" Paul asked rationally as he guided the boat across the water.

"Well, just in case," Mary muttered and tried to hide a smile. She was beginning to realize how absurd her words sounded.

"Just in case," Suzie agreed.

Chapter Eight

As the boat skimmed across the water the sun was beginning to set. Suzie's heart swelled at the peaceful slope of the sky against the sea. In her mind she pieced together the last moments of Alexandria's life. She had been running from Al and George. She had probably known that if they caught her, they would be able to force the truth out of her, and then all the prison time that Darren was doing would be pointless. Worse than that they might have even killed her. But George and Al had pursued her right up to the edge of the cliff.

Alexandria had turned back to see where they were, just as George lunged for her. She had jumped after all, but not because she wanted to die. She had jumped because she was trying to escape from George and Al and the torture they promised her. She had jumped because she was trying to protect her husband, even though he had failed to protect her.

Suzie sighed as she tried to comprehend how a young woman could be so blinded by love that she was prepared to bury the proceeds of a crime. She must have known that keeping a map of where the money was buried was a risk but it was obviously a risk she was prepared to take so Darren could find the buried money if something ever happened to her.

It truly was a sad story, but one that would finally have an ending. It might not be happy, but at least it was true. The money, once found, would be returned to its rightful owners and the two men who had caused her death, would be behind bars for a long time. She sighed as she felt the tension in her muscles begin to slowly unwind. By the time they arrived at the docks, she was feeling as if she was a million miles away from the frightening experience she had just survived. Mary was eager to get off the boat, but Suzie lingered for a moment.

"Are you coming, Suzie?" Mary called over her

shoulder. "Jason asked us to meet him at the station, remember?"

"I remember," Suzie replied reluctantly. The sun was just beginning to sink lower in the sky and with its descent a myriad of pinks and deep oranges had sprouted across the blue expanse.

"You can stay, if you want," Paul offered as he finished tying the boat to the dock. He glanced up at her, and Suzie caught his eye as she smiled.

"I'd like that," she said quietly. "But what about Jason?"

"Don't worry about Jason," Mary said knowingly. "I'll take care of him."

"Thanks," Suzie called out as Mary hurried off along the docks. Suzie got the feeling that Mary was happy to give her and Paul some alone time.

Paul rested his arms gently against the railing of the boat and smiled faintly at her. Suzie could feel his gaze skimming across her features but she was too nervous to look in his direction. It was the strangest thing for her. She had never been nervous with any man before. She couldn't understand why it was so difficult to even talk to Paul without her heart acting wild and her mind spinning. She felt more than a little foolish.

"Suzie," he murmured, his voice drifting as seamlessly as the waves that rolled gently against the boat.

"Hmm?" Suzie inquired without looking in his direction.

"Suzie," he repeated and rested his hand lightly along the curve of the back of her hand. "Am I making you uncomfortable?" he asked, his voice still soft. "Did you want to be alone?"

"No," Suzie replied and forced herself to look into his clear gray eyes. "I'm sorry, Paul. I guess, I'm just a little," she hesitated a moment and then admitted in a whisper. "Nervous."

"Nervous?" his smile grew and for the first time she noticed the way his eyes lit up to a bluish shade when he was amused. "What's there to be nervous about?" he asked.

Suzie lowered her eyes and felt the heat rising in her cheeks. She took a slow deep breath and tried to convince herself that she was being silly, that they were just two friends enjoying the water and the view. When she felt his fingertips reach up to lightly trace along her cheek, and the gentle swoop of him tucking her hair back behind her ear, the warmth from his touch spread throughout her body. She glanced over at him shyly.

"Is it this?" he asked and leaned a little closer to her, his lips puckered just slightly in anticipation of a kiss. Suzie only had a split-second to decide what she was going to do. All of her desire was to allow the kiss, but all of her instincts told her to be cautious. Just as his lips would have brushed hers, she tilted her head slightly to the side so that he grazed only the corner of her mouth. He lightly pecked her cheek, and then pulled away. Suzie glanced back up at him guiltily, expecting him to be hurt or even angry, but instead he was smiling whimsically at her.

"I'm sorry," she murmured as she searched his eyes.

"I'm patient," he replied with a wink before looking back out over the water. Something about his words left Suzie feeling even more comfortable with him than she had before. She laid her hand lightly over his and they continued to gaze out over the water.

There was a lot about Garber that was new for her, but the most surprising thing had to be the way that Paul made her feel. Awkward and silly, but so very content when she was beside him. She leaned a little closer to him, and he naturally draped his arm around her shoulder, pulling her gently against him. She offered a subtle sigh as she rested her head lightly against the crook of his shoulder. Across the scattered colors of the setting sun, a flock of birds flew. Suzie felt her spirit soar in time with their rise through the clouds. It was a moment she was certain she would treasure.

The End

More Cozy Mysteries by Cindy Bell

Dune House Cozy Mystery Series

Seaside Secrets

Boats and Bad Guys

Heavenly Highland Inn Cozy Mystery Series

Murdering the Roses

Dead in the Daisies

Killing the Carnations

Drowning the Daffodils

Suffocating the Sunflowers

Wendy the Wedding Planner Cozy Mystery Series

Matrimony, Money and Murder

Chefs, Ceremonies and Crimes

Bekki the Beautician Cozy Mystery Series

Hairspray and Homicide

A Dyed Blonde and a Dead Body

Mascara and Murder

Pageant and Poison

Conditioner and a Corpse

Mistletoe, Makeup and Murder

Hairpin, Hair Dryer and Homicide

Blush, a Bride and a Body

Shampoo and a Stiff

Cosmetics, a Cruise and a Killer

Lipstick, a Long Iron and Lifeless

Printed in Great Britain
by Amazon